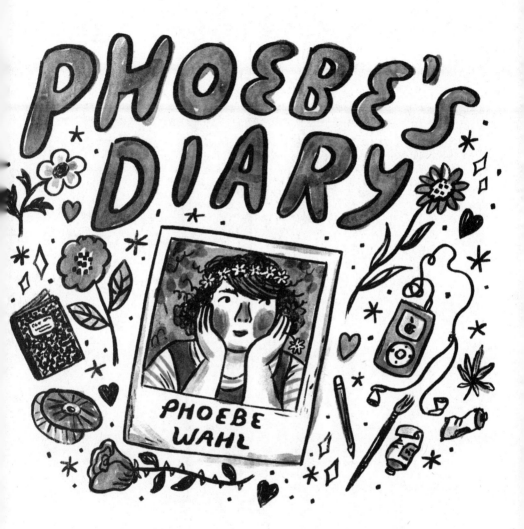

PHOEBE'S DIARY

PHOEBE WAHL

LITTLE, BROWN AND COMPANY

New York Boston

Copyright © 2023 by Phoebe Wahl

Cover art copyright © 2023 by Phoebe Wahl
Cover design by Sasha Illingworth and Patrick Hulse
Cover copyright © 2023 by Hachette Book Group, Inc.

Little, Brown and Company
Hachette Book Group
1290 Avenue of the Americas, New York, NY 10104
Visit us at LBYR.com

First Edition: September 2023

Little, Brown and Company is a division of Hachette Book Group, Inc. The Little, Brown name and logo are trademarks of Hachette Book Group, Inc.

The publisher is not responsible for websites (or their content) that are not owned by the publisher.

Little, Brown and Company books may be purchased in bulk for business, educational, or promotional use. For information, please contact your local bookseller or the Hachette Book Group Special Markets Department at special.markets@hbgusa.com.

Library of Congress Cataloging-in-Publication Data
Names: Wahl, Phoebe, author, illustrator.
Title: Phoebe's diary / Phoebe Wahl.
Description: First edition. | New York : Little, Brown and Company, 2023. | Audience: Ages 14 & up. | Summary: "Drawing on her own diaries, Phoebe Wahl presents the illustrated journal of a teenage girl careening through the turmoil and ecstasy of adolescence amid school plays, art projects, favorite bands, blossoming friendships, and new love." —Provided by publisher.
Identifiers: LCCN 2022004064 | ISBN 9780316363563 (hardcover) | ISBN 9780316363853 (ebook)
Subjects: CYAC: Diaries—Fiction. | LCGFT: Diary fiction.
Classification: LCC PZ7.1.W3452 Ph 2023 | DDC [Fic]—dc23
LC record available at https://lccn.loc.gov/2022004064

ISBNs: 978-0-316-36356-3 (hardcover), 978-0-316-36385-3 (ebook)

Printed in the United States of America

LAKE

10 9 8 7 6 5 4 3 2

For DH. Thank you
for diving back into this
world with me, and cheering
me on every step of the way.

For Jenn & Susan, with
thanks for your unwavering
confidence & enthusiasm.

And for my family,
with apologies...!

THURSDAY, JULY 20, 2006, 4:10 P.M.

It is exactly one week until opening night of the summer play, *The Night Thoreau Spent in Jail*. It is ridiculously hot here, in the 80s I think, but I actually have no idea and totally made that up....I've mostly been sitting at the computer today, but now I'm up in my room drawing and getting headaches from the heat. I'm hiding out from Dad, who keeps giving me grief about "lazing around" inside all day while it's so nice out.

Keeping a diary is something I haven't done in a long time, mostly because I forget to write in it once, and then again, and then I neglect it for months or years, and by the time I come back, everything is old news and no longer interests me.

I wish I was better at sticking with things. I never finish stories I write. Instead I just replay them in my mind millions of times, I become obsessed and think that THIS story apart from any other story will be the one I'm satisfied with, or the one I even just come up with an ending for. But I can never come up with endings. And I'm never happy with what I make. I always get critical or move on to some new idea. You'd think a diary would be different, since it's just everyday life, but my track record isn't good. So hopefully this journal will be the exception, since it would be nice to follow through for once.

I'm afraid of how hot it's going to be on our trip. We're leaving in a week and a half, right after the summer play ends, for a family road trip to Montana. What if I get heatstroke like I did the time Roxie and I sat at the park for hours while Mom hosted her harmonizing workshop at our house, and I almost passed out on the bike ride home? Plus, Roxie will probably mock me because I'm not tan, and because my only swimsuit is a one-piece.

I barely ate anything today too, which might be contributing to the headache. I just wasn't very hungry…maybe it's the heat. Or because I'm nervous about the first performance of the play. OR that I'm dreading our family road trip…or maybe the fact that I'm desperately in love…

Torn, between three different men.

4:42 P.M.

I AM feeling nervous about the play, though. I'm afraid of people being better than me. I get so jealous of the other actors. It's the same way with my art. I even got jealous of the old people in the figure-drawing class I took last year, who had about 60 years more practice than I did.

Everyone always "raves" about what a "good artist" and actor I am, but I know I'm not, compared to a lot of people who are even just a few years older than me....Everyone who is in the play has acted before. And it's true a lot of them are juniors and seniors, but even the other people my age, like Nora and Nathan, were in the school plays last year as freshmen, if only just as chorus. I was in drama class but was too nervous to audition for any plays until the summer came around...even though my teacher, Ms. Hanley, was always encouraging me to. Ugh, what have I gotten myself into? Maybe I should pretend this headache turns into the bubonic plague so I can't perform.

AH YES, IT'S AN ACUTE CASE OF CANNOT POSSIBLY DO THIS PLAY.

ANYWAY. The first object of my love is Owen McCloud.

Here is what I know about Owen McCloud. He's 16 and lives in the cohousing community down by the creek, which means there's a good chance our families know each other through the hippie grapevine.

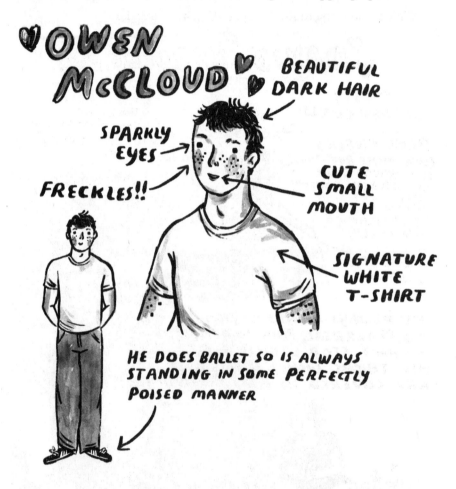

♥ OWEN McCLOUD ♥

BEAUTIFUL DARK HAIR

SPARKLY EYES →

FRECKLES!! →

CUTE SMALL MOUTH

SIGNATURE WHITE T-SHIRT

HE DOES BALLET SO IS ALWAYS STANDING IN SOME PERFECTLY POISED MANNER

He's always finding excuses to sit next to me during rehearsal and laughs when I laugh. He makes a lot of eye contact. I like him better than David...for the moment. There's such an intensity about David, I can't tell what he's thinking. Owen seems more honest, and relatable.

Plus, he's only a year older than me (he'll be a junior this fall). And David will be a senior, which does feel a little out of my league.

Which brings me to love interest #2, David Berglund.

♥ DAVID BERGLUND ♥

MESSY GOLDEN CURLS

GREEN EYES GAZING THOUGHTFULLY INTO THE DISTANCE

PINK CHEEKS (LIKE MINE BUT LESS "RUDDY COOK IN A DICKENS NOVEL" AND MORE "WINDSWEPT GENTLEMAN ON A HORSE")

ROGUISH SMILE

HE ALWAYS WEARS SHORTS TO REHEARSAL, AND SOMETIMES I CAN'T STOP LOOKING AT HIS THIGHS, WHICH ARE THICK AND COVERED IN FINE BLOND HAIR.

(ONCE HIS SHORTS WERE BAGGY ENOUGH THAT I COULD ALMOST SEE DOWN THEM AND I HAD TO FORCE MYSELF TO LOOK AWAY.)

David is ridiculously smart. Last night I read all his blogs on Myspace.

They were so philosophical and deep that I had to read each post about 15 times before I understood what he was talking about. But nonetheless I found myself kind of falling in love with his words....He also has lots of outdoorsy pictures on his profile....I'm a bit intimidated by his wholesome nature-y-ness actually. What if we did start dating, and he was such a mountain-man sage that he could never really BE with me? What if he loved shrubs and beavers more than me? What if he expected me to, like...scale Everest with him but I wasn't in good enough shape and he just left me huffing and puffing in the snow?

At rehearsal recently he said, "You did really good today" (or something of that nature). I was surprised, partly because he'd never talked to me before, and because I only have a small role and there isn't really any chance to do much intense acting. I said, "Thanks, you did good too" (which he did) and he said, "Thanks."

Maybe he's too shy to talk to me, even though he doesn't seem like a shy person around anyone else....I think maybe I like him more than Owen....

Love interest #3 is Lukas Viitala....

Lukas is less of a factor actually...because he's just so out of my league. And I think he likes Mari. Everyone likes Mari. And it doesn't help that she plays his love interest in the play.

I play his mother—so he's already predisposed to see me as more of a matronly teapot than a female human with sex appeal. Although he does kiss me on the cheek in the play. But it's more of a mother-son peck....It WAS my first cheek kiss, though (from someone outside my family). But I didn't tell him that. I made it seem like I get kissed on the cheek by Scandinavian-sex-god seniors all the time.

♥ LUKAS VIITALA ♥

SHAGGY GOLDEN-BROWN HAIR THAT FALLS IN FRONT OF HIS FACE

KISSABLE LIPS

FINLAND SHIRT— HIS PARENTS ARE FROM THERE, SO HE CAN SPEAK FINNISH *HOT*

SCRAPES & BRUISES FROM A SKATEBOARD ACCIDENT A FEW WEEKS AGO *HOT*

SUOMI

Lukas is always nice to me but we barely interact outside the scenes we're in together....He generally hangs out with the other seniors—Mari, David, and Annie—during rehearsals.

I wish I could skateboard so we'd have something to talk about. Once I stood on Roxie's longboard for like three seconds and fell off. He'd probably like her better since she's into skateboarding and more his type: petite, thin, and cool. I asked if she knew him and she said they had Spanish class together. So he can speak three languages. HOT.

Anyway. I don't think he'll ever like me, but a girl can dream, right?

Friday, July 21, 5:07 p.m.

Owen likes me. I think.

Actually, I have no idea, but it's my secret suspicion he does.

Which isn't even secret, because I shared it with Roxie. She didn't know who he was, even when I showed her his picture in the yearbook. She probably thinks I'm kidding myself that he could like me, but at least she's humoring me, for now.

Today it was pouring rain, and everyone came to my house to rehearse. We usually practice in Mari Blume's yard, because it's big and open enough for us to do our blocking (since it's the summer play, we're not on the school stage). But because of the rain we needed to be indoors, and Mari couldn't find her key and her parents weren't home, so we were locked out. Ms. Hanley, our director, said, "Does anyone else live nearby? Looks like we need a different practice spot today." Mari lives right next to me, so I suggested everyone go to my house. My heart was pounding because I was nervous at the thought. But I knew it might be my only chance in history to have cool, popular people over, like Annie and Lukas (aka the most utterly beautiful human you will ever witness) and David and Owen (not too shabby themselves). Plus, I wanted to save the day.

11

As we left Mari's, Owen said, "Where's your house?"

I said, "Down there," and pointed through the trees. I asked whether he thought we should take the trail or the road. Owen said, "Let's brave the outdoors," and smiled his adorable smile. I didn't have the heart to point out that the road was also outdoors. So down the trail we went.

It felt funny leading Mari down the trail, as if we hadn't scrambled down it a million times together. Before Mari was the cool, popular queen of the Thespians that she is today, we were friends as kids. Our moms met working together at Planned Parenthood in the 80s or something, and then Mari's family moved in next door. She was home-schooled like us, so she and Roxie and I would play together almost every day growing up. What we did isn't the kind of homeschooling most people think of when they hear the word—everyone is always surprised Roxie and I aren't, like, backwoods evangelical extremists or reclusive, hard-core intellectuals. Our homeschooling was on the more relaxed, lefty side of things…no curriculums, no homework, no real structure at all. I was a "kindergarten dropout," as Mom likes to say. I started like everyone else when I was five but immediately hated it because there wasn't enough time to draw, and my parents said Roxie and I were "losing our sparks" (she was in fourth grade when we left). So, Mom started reading all kinds of books about radical unschooling and decided to pull us out. At home, "school" basically consisted of drawing all day and playing outside for hours on end. Most people can't believe it when I tell them I did whatever I wanted every day and are so surprised we don't have zero social skills. But it's not like we were being cloistered away in some remote cave.

Roxie and Mari and I would put on plays for our families, record pretend radio shows on cassette tapes, and go on all kinds of hikes and

MARI BLUME

field trips, like to the science center in Vancouver, or to the Seattle Art Museum, or midnight clamming on the beach with Dad.

Since Roxie is the oldest, she was always the leader, and Mari was kind of the second-in-command.

In summertime, we'd meet up early in the morning and play together all day with the other kids in the neighborhood, making forts and picking plums and playing sardines or hide-and-go-seek in and out of neighbors' yards.

That's when we bushwhacked the trail through the blackberry-covered bank below Mari's house, and it became a permanent path. It comes out at the top of our driveway, making the perfect shortcut between our houses.

I still take it sometimes to go up to her house for rehearsal. But she probably forgot it even exists. Or is at least pretending like it in front of everyone else. A relic of when she was uncool enough to have been friends with me. Everything started falling apart when Roxie and Mari both decided to go back to public school, Mari for seventh grade and Roxie for high school. Roxie started to get too cool, and Mari started making other friends. It just got awkward and I was kind of left behind. The family gatherings kept going but they weren't the same. Mari would bring a book and read quietly in the corner, and Roxie would disappear into her room.

I'm sure Mari would die if the other people in the play found out our families are so close.

Last year, when I decided to start high school part time, I was secretly hoping Mari and I could be friends again, but she didn't talk to me. She's only

ONCE ROXIE EVEN ROPED US INTO PERFORMING "RIVERDANCE" DURING HER MICHAEL FLATLEY PHASE.

started to a little bit now that we're in the play. I bet her mom said she had to be nice to me or else.

7:45 p.m.

Sorry, had to go eat dinner.

ANYHOO…Owen and I were kind of alone, ahead of everyone else going down the trail. The most alone we've ever been, since usually there's other people around at rehearsal. We didn't say anything to each other, but it wasn't an awkward silence, just a silence. My legs were shaking as I walked because I was nervous about falling on my ass on the muddy trail in front of Owen, who was loping gracefully down the path with his hands in his pockets, like some kind of goddamn forest elf.

FRIZZED-OUT HAIR FROM THE RAIN

SOAKED JEANS, I HOPE HE DOESN'T THINK I PEED MY PANTS !!!

I kept being surprised at how close he was behind me. Ms. Hanley and the rest of the cast were all a ways behind us on the trail. Wouldn't he hang back with them if he DIDN'T like me? Was he excited to go to my house???

I thought about running ahead to hide any pictures of Roxie, so he didn't realize I had a cooler, prettier, older sister and decide to like her instead....

Every time I'd glance back at him, he'd just smile, the same smile he gives me whenever I catch his eye at rehearsals. It looks kind of like, "Hi, it's just me." And it makes my heart skip. It's SO hard to break eye contact whenever we make it, it's like I'm being sucked into a vortex of blue and can't look away. Must. Keep. Eyes. On. Path. So. I. Don't. Fall. On. My. Ass.

When we got to my house, Owen was looking all around, and that was another thing that made me think he likes me. Because he was acting a bit like *I* would act if I was in the house of someone *I* like, just quietly taking everything in. He stared at some of my paintings on the wall, and I wondered if he knew I made them. Throughout rehearsal, he sat on two different chairs and a stool, and I wondered if he was trying to sit on as many pieces of MY furniture as possible. He asked if he could have a glass of water, and I wondered if he wanted to touch MY glasses and drink MY water. And of course, I wondered if I was imagining everything. If I was taking the very smallest hints and running wild with them, just like I always do, because I want it SO badly to be true that he likes me.

He probably just thinks I'm

ITEMS THAT HAVE
TOUCHED OWEN'S BUTT
AND LIPS (!!!)

16

a nice person, or a good actor and artist, and wants to be my friend. Maybe he's one of those overly nice people who make you think they like you because they're just so kind and genuine…like maybe he knows I like him and he's humoring me out of pity, and because he's too nice to turn me down.

Ugh, how embarrassing.

It's best to keep my hopes down, because it's always when I'm not expecting it that exciting things happen.

Mari acted like she'd never even been to my house. Like her family doesn't come over every year for Hanukkah and New Year's and Passover.

Before dinner I tried to find the glass HE (Owen) drank out of earlier so I could use it too. Then it would almost be like we had kissed.

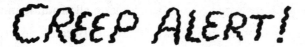

But Mom had already put it in the dishwasher.

Saturday, July 22, 12:05 a.m.

Just got in bed. I went out with Roxie because there was an outdoor movie going in the park, which means a good chance of seeing our crushes (Owen, David, Lukas for me, and that hipster boy with the snakes for Roxie)....

She saw the snake guy, but we concluded he probably has a girlfriend, because we saw him with this waifish girl in skinny jeans who we've seen him with one time before. I wish I had skinny jeans. Roxie altered hers to be skinnier, she said she'd do mine too.

I didn't see any of my crushes, not even Owen, who was the highest probability since he lives in this part of town. But my heart rate was spiked the whole time we were out anyway, as if one of them was going to come around a corner at any moment. Roxie said I should just invite Owen out sometime. As if that's just a THING. But I couldn't bear to make the first move when I'm so unsure if he likes me.

We ended up wandering around well after the sun went down, which isn't till about 10 p.m. this time of year. Roxie had her longboard and was skating down the empty streets near the elementary school, which made me nervous even though there was no one out.

I felt cool being out so late with Roxie skate-boarding, I wished I had a joint to smoke or something. I just feel like being bad. I'm tired of being the little sister and matronly teapot mother character.

I think Roxie has smoked pot. Sometimes I can tell she sprays perfume or hair spray in her room just to cover up the smell of something else, and she's all spacey and her eyes are red.

YEAH? WHAT OF IT, BITCH?

I know Owen has, because he told me once he went out to one of Jenna Thompson's parties at her family's lake house, and I've heard everyone drinks and smokes pot at those.

Jenna Thompson is one of the cast members of the play. She plays Lydian, Ralph Waldo Emerson's wife/Thoreau's slight romantic interest. If she wasn't so friendly, I probably would hate her, because she is so perfect.

She's a junior, lives out on the

SHINY, LUXURIOUS TRESSES →

ADORABLE DIMPLES AND GLAMOROUS BEAUTY MARK??! UNFAIR.

JENNA THOMPSON

lake, in a mansion I think, and drives a retro
VW bug to school. She is good friends with
Owen and Sam, who are in her year. There
is a rumor that she and Owen had some kind
of "thing" last summer. I heard from Annie, who
heard it from David, who heard it from Owen himself.

She said she thought it was kind of a "friends with benefits" situation.

I can't help but wonder if they had sex or not....I bet they didn't. But
I'm probably just deluding myself because I want his first time to be
with me....Ha! I AM worried that he still likes her. He probably does.
Because who wouldn't. Most of the guys either like her or Mari.

I can't even imagine a world in which Mom and Dad wouldn't know if I snuck out in the middle of the night and didn't come back till morning. Our stairs are too creaky! What do they do, jump out their windows with parachutes???

Plus Mom would absolutely flip if I ever went to Post Point at night. You have to walk way down the railroad tracks along the beach to get there, and it's where all the mega-stoners go to hop freights and play bongos.

Annie is one of the chorus members in our play, and she is the main purveyor of gossip. She has a giant crush on David Berglund and everyone knows it. They're also best friends and are always sneaking smoke breaks during *Thoreau* rehearsals when they're not in a scene. She is equal parts annoying and endearing. She is always the loudest and snarkiest and is always making awkward sexual innuendos and trying as much as

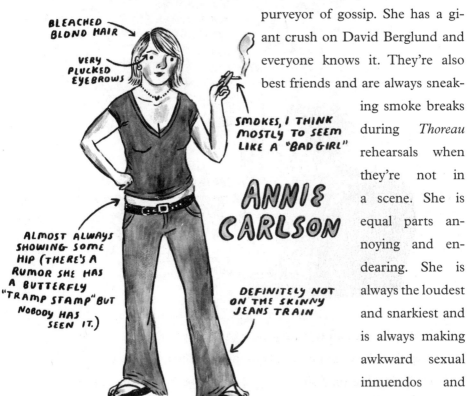

BLEACHED BLOND HAIR

VERY PLUCKED EYEBROWS

SMOKES, I THINK MOSTLY TO SEEM LIKE A "BAD GIRL"

ANNIE CARLSON

ALMOST ALWAYS SHOWING SOME HIP (THERE'S A RUMOR SHE HAS A BUTTERFLY "TRAMP STAMP" BUT NOBODY HAS SEEN IT.)

DEFINITELY NOT ON THE SKINNY JEANS TRAIN

she can to broadcast all the "things" she's done or wants to do. She can be really funny, though. Mostly she just likes to act too cool, and better than everyone else. It's like she's either "on," being really funny and wild, OR super cold and checked out smoking in the corner. She's one of the first theater people I met. We were in drama class second semester together last year, and she was kind of obsessed with me.

At first she didn't ever talk to me but then friended me on Myspace and started leaving me 180,000,000 picture and site comments about how much she liked my style and how good at acting I was.

It's like she wanted to be my best friend, but then when we were in class together she didn't even talk to me very often, just online.

But during the play she's started to be nicer. Maybe because I'm more part of the official group now, like I've proved myself or something.

Yesterday at rehearsal Annie invited me to one of Jenna's parties.

Eye roll. I'm not even a freshman anymore, now that school is out!
Owen heard her and he said, "Don't listen to her. The parties are fun,
though, you should come!" Sigh. He's so nice. And cute. And perfect in
every goddamn way.

Jenna's parties are like the kind you hear about or see in movies about teenagers. With kegs and red plastic cups, where everyone is smoking weed and making out. At least that's what I imagine from what I've heard. If Owen said I should come, that means he wants me there, right?

BUT of course, Jenna's party is the weekend after the play, when I'll be on vacation with my family. Just my luck. Probably my only chance for anything to happen with any of the guys I like for the whole summer, and I'll be stuck in our Toyota Sienna in, like, the middle of Montana looking out the window at buffalo.

I know Owen is going. He's been talking about it. So are David, Mari, Lukas, and everyone in the entire cast, except Nora I bet.

Nora is the one person who, besides Owen, I hang out with at rehearsals most. She is kind of the reason I'm in the play at all. Like Annie, she was in my drama class last year too, and we started to become friends. When Ms. Hanley first started encouraging me to try out for the plays, Nora was really supportive. She introduced me to the whole drama crew at auditions. She is also in my year, which makes her automatically less intimidating, even though she has more theater experience than me. She's super introverted, but once you hang out for a while you realize she has a really dry, sarcastic sense of humor. We have a LOT in common. Mostly nerdy things like our love for all things Harry Potter and Lord of the Rings. I'm hoping this summer we can hang out more and get closer, because I feel like she might have best-friend potential, and I feel like I haven't had one in oh so long.

GLASSES (DORKY AND NOT STYLISH, BUT I'LL FORGIVE HER)

LONG, GLORIOUS HAIR LIKE EOWYN FROM LORD OF THE RINGS, BUT RED *

FRIENDLY BUT SHY SMILE

THEATER T-SHIRT OF SOME KIND

NORA WINTERS

FLOPPY SHOULDER BAG OF BOOKS (SHE'S ALWAYS READING.)

CONVERSE

* I WISH MY HAIR COULD GROW THAT LONG. IT SEEMS TO STOP AT NIPPLE - LENGTH

The other boys in the play are Sam Goldman and Nathan Stone. Sam is nice but also very serious. Sometimes I feel like he's judging me when Owen and I are talking too much, or when I'm getting carried away being rowdy with Annie or whispering with Nora during rehearsal. He's a junior, and good friends with Owen, so maybe he thinks I'm some intruder strumpet trying to steal his friend away. He plays

SAM GOLDMAN

John Thoreau, Henry's brother who dies from lockjaw. We don't interact much, even though I play his mother in the show. He would be hot, except that he has a weird triangular bob and is always wearing something strange and unstylish, like a bowler hat or shoes with square-ular toes.

Nathan is in my year, and lives in my neighborhood. His mom is a local celebrity because she's in a Beatles cover band that plays at Mari's family's giant summer solstice party every year. He's a big film geek and works at Trek Video, so I always see him there. We used to do that weird nod of "we've known each other our whole lives

NATHAN STONE

but don't really interact ever so we'll just vaguely acknowledge each other's existence and not talk" kind of thing, but now that I'm in the play, when I go in there, we say hi.

P.S.

I forgot to say before—DAVID commented on one of my Myspace photos....

He said "Classy" on the photo of me at the Eiffel Tower on our family trip to France last summer!!!!!!!!!!!!!!!!!!!!!!

I wish the flash hadn't made my eyes light up like some kind of psychic devil in that picture!!! And I can only pray that he didn't go through the rest of the album and see the hilarious-but-immature photos of Roxie and me at the Louvre, or Dad on the beach trying to "blend in with the locals."

MONDAY, JULY 24, 9:46 A.M.

Four days until opening night. I haven't performed in an actual play in years (if you even count the crappy ones from kids' theater camp) and I'm afraid I'll forget everything.

It is still fucking blistering hot out....Not a fan, as in I don't enjoy it, but there is also no fan.

I miss David Berglund after not having had rehearsals all weekend...and Owen too. Lukas...not so much. I think my crush on him is waning—he just seems so much less attainable.

Anyhoo, I'm going to Costco with Mom now, 'cause I'm cool like that.

Rehearsal this afternoon!

12:01 P.M.

SOMETIMES, WHEN I'M ALONE IN MY ROOM, I SCOOT ALL THE WAY TO THE EDG OF MY BED AND TRY TO PRESS MYSELF AS CLOSE TO THE WALL AS I CAN. THAT WA IT'S LIKE THERE'S ROOM FOR SOMEONE ELSE, AND I IMAGINE WHAT IT WOUL BE LIKE TO HAVE OWEN IN MY BED.
OR DAVID.

Sometimes I want someone, ANYONE, so badly that I want to run and shout. Someone that I know would love me, someone who could fill that empty half of my bed. I know it seems silly, and like a high school cliché, but it feels so real. Too real, sometimes. I can't stop thinking about David. I see him in about two hours.

I'm ready to have a summer fling, or even a full-blown relationship. I feel like I've waited long enough, longer than most people. I'm fifteen for god's sake, and I've never been kissed, never been anywhere close to being kissed for real.

11:05 *p.m.*

It is my half birthday today. I'm exactly fifteen and a half. It didn't make my day any better, however. I saw David at play practice, and he didn't say anything, which isn't unusual since he's kind of quiet, and had never really talked to me before. I don't know why I thought it would be different, just because he commented on my Myspace photo. For some reason, I felt like he was avoiding me, and I don't know why he would be.

Owen wasn't there today. Maybe he's sick.

Today was a lonely day.

P.S.

I remembered one good thing that happened today, which is that Roxie made my jeans into SKINNY JEANS with her serger.

FINALLY!!

WEDNESDAY, JULY 26, 10:25 A.M.

my COSTUME

Today is our first dress rehearsal.

Yesterday, at practice, David didn't talk to me again, so I distracted myself with Owen, who was back. I think it's more likely that Owen likes me. He's always nice. I love how he's covered in freckles. I noticed how his arms are starting to get tan after rehearsing every day outside in Mari's yard.

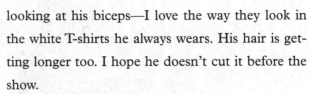

Sometimes I can't stop looking at his biceps—I love the way they look in the white T-shirts he always wears. His hair is getting longer too. I hope he doesn't cut it before the show.

Last night I dreamed David passed me a note. I don't remember what it said but I was in love. I dreamed I was overwhelmingly happy. I want to be overwhelmingly happy.

FRIDAY, JULY 28, 8:50 A.M.

The first show was last night. It was sold out, oversold out, because there were only supposed to be 100 people and there were 130, so everyone was sitting on the floor really close to us and it was like 300 degrees, especially in the tiny backstage area where we were all crammed together. When we did our preshow-huddle pep talk, I got to be right up against Owen. My arm was around his waist, and his was over my shoulder. On my other side, I was in Lukas's armpit practically because he's so tall. We were all dying from the heat but being next to Owen still felt nice. He smells good, salty, like sweat but also sweet and flowery and like Old Spice deodorant.

Owen and I have entrances close to one another, and from the same side of the stage, so we're often waiting right behind the curtain together, our hearts pounding as we're about to go on. Now that we're performing for an actual audience, we have to whisper any back-stage conversation we're having, which means we have to lean close. Close enough to feel his breath on my temple as he talks.

He's so smiley, and always seems genuinely interested in what I have to say, and he asks questions. If I wasn't falling in love with him, I might think it was weird how utterly sociable he is compared to other boys.

I don't have any of the same entrances as David, and we're not in any of the same scenes, and so now that rehearsals are over, I haven't interacted with him much. But I find myself not even caring. All I can think about is Owen.

All of a sudden, it doesn't seem like pure fantasy that he might like me too. It seems kind of real. And I'm afraid, because I'm only going to see him about twice more, and then I leave on our family trip, and what if he stops liking me? Or I stop loving him? What if I don't see him again until school starts, and he forgets about me completely, or is embarrassed to like me because once we're out of the world of the summer play, he realizes I'm not actually that cool?

4:27 p.m.

Mom drives me so wild I can't stand it. Everything she says…I just itch to run out of the house screaming and never come back. Lately Roxie has been getting on my nerves too. It's like she never really takes me seriously.

11:35 P.M.

The second show was today. It went really well, all sold out again. And I'm in love with Owen. We talked a lot today, about music and our summers and the play....Before the show, he was asking me how his makeup was and all of a sudden, I realized we were flirting. It just never felt like I thought flirting would—it felt natural, like we were just talking. Is it glaringly obvious to everyone else that we like each other? I think David has noticed, unless I'm imagining it. He gives me funny looks when Owen and I are talking. Maybe he's sore that I haven't really been paying any attention to him now that shows have started. Tomorrow is the last show, and the second to last day before I leave. I don't want to go. I don't want the play to be over. I want to live for at least another week in the tiny backstage of the theater, packed in with the whole cast, talking to Owen and getting that rush of adrenaline right before going onstage, feeling the warmth of the lights and seeing all the people.

After the show tomorrow there is talk of all going out to Kendrick's billiards hall. I'm worried because I don't know how to play pool. I told Owen and he said, "I'll have to teach you."
Perhaps he will give me a ride...?

Perhaps...at the last curtain call, he'll dip me back and kiss me, and we'll write postcards to each other for the rest of the summer....

But actually, I wouldn't want that to happen in front of all those people. Maybe just a quick kiss backstage, after the show...both of us giddy after the release of so much tension and nervous energy...OR perhaps I'll go home after the show, nothing will happen, and I won't see him until school.

I'm anxious to go out after the show with Annie and Mari and Lukas and everyone cool. It will be my first time hanging out with them outside rehearsal. And even though we all feel like friends after this weekend of shows (even Mari...), I still have this fear that some spell will be broken once the play is over, that everyone will realize I'm just a nerdy young (almost) sophomore and that I don't actually belong in their friend group outside of the play....

Sunday, July 30, 8:50 a.m.

Last night's show was amazing. We were all trembling afterward. I can't believe it's over. After curtain call, when we all ran outside to greet people, Owen hugged me. He kind of enveloped me, almost lifted me off the ground, he hugged me so hard. His body was warm and damp from sweat. I didn't see him hug anyone else like that.

After getting out of costume we all went to get ice cream, and somehow, I got a ride with Owen.

His dad was there after the show, and so first we drove with him back

OWEN'S HOUSE (!!!)

to their house so his dad could stay at home and we could take the car. I got to see his house briefly, from the outside. Every time I drive past the cohousing community with Mom, I wonder which one it is, and now I know. It's blue, and there are lots of plants growing outside.

As we drove to get ice cream we mostly talked about music. Owen likes some indie music like I do, Modest Mouse and the Shins, but mostly hip-hop like Blue Scholars and the Fugees. We talked about how Blue Scholars are going to be at Bumbershoot this fall, along with Metric and Spoon. I don't really listen to Spoon, but I pretended I did.

Sometimes there was silence while we drove, and that was okay. I always have to remind myself that silence is okay and that the world won't combust if I don't say something for one second. It felt funny just leaving the theater alone with him and showing up at Mallard Ice Cream together. I wondered what everyone thought, and if they noticed. If he and Jenna really did have a "fling" last summer, did she notice? Was she jealous? David gave me funny looks all night, and Mari kept smiling at me. Sometimes David would interrupt Owen's and my conversation and just start talking to me, more than he ever has before. While Owen and I were in the middle of a conversation, he asked me if I'd ever been to the boutique in Fairhaven called the Paperdoll. I said yes, and then he just wanted to talk about shopping.

Then later, when we were all walking over to Kendrick's, I was walking ahead of the group with Owen, and David came up and said, "Do you like my shirt?" and started talking about clothes.

I felt like David was realizing that Owen and I really liked each other and was trying to kind of compete for my attention, which was strange.

At Kendrick's, Owen taught me how to play pool. I sucked but it was okay because he was so nice. I felt like everyone was watching, but maybe it was all in my head.

AT ONE POINT, HE STOOD
BEHIND ME, HIS BODY
PRESSING UP AGAINST MY BACK, AND
HIS ARM AND HAND OVER MINE
SHOWING ME THE BEST WAY
TO SHOOT (!!!!!)

When people were heading home, he asked if I had a ride home. I said no even though I could have gotten rides with Nathan or Mari, both of whom live right near me.

We said goodbye to everyone as we parted ways, walking just the two of us to where his car was parked. It felt so natural, like we were a couple, and I wondered again what people thought. My heart rate kicked up a notch at this point, because it all just felt so surreal. Like literally exactly what I wrote that I hoped would happen a few days ago! Well, not the backstage kiss, but the ride, the time alone with him.

WHEN WE GOT INTO HIS CAR, HE SAID,

(MEANING MY NUMBER ... !!!!)

He seemed really nervous, kind of like he'd been planning to ask all night. I noticed that his hands were shaking
as he put my number into his flip phone. I got his too.

We drove over the hill through the WWU campus to get home, talking
and laughing and listening to music. Then, it started raining and we
rolled down our windows and talked about how much we love rain.

The air wafting in had that
particular sweet scent of
summer rain on warm as-
phalt, and the drops com-
ing in felt like cool sparks
hitting my warm cheeks.
Everything felt like a perfect dream.

As we came over the hill
toward my house, he
asked if I minded if he
called Sam. I didn't because I thought it would only last a moment. But
he drew out their conversation, asking all kinds of random questions
about what Sam was up to now and whether he was going to hang out
with one of their other friends out at Post Point or not. As we got closer
to my house my heart began to sink, because not only did it seem like
he and some of the other cast members had plans to hang out more
(without me) tonight, but it was clear that he was still going to be on
the phone talking mundane ride and meetup plans with Sam when he
dropped me off.

When we got to my house, he stopped the car, saying "Just a minute" to Sam on the phone. And then, for what felt like the first time with him, it was really awkward. Because there we were, idling at the top of my driveway. We'd been flirting all night, all weekend, and it had felt like it was all building up to this. Him teaching me pool, asking if I needed a ride, asking for my NUMBER, and now nothing was going to happen. Because Sam was waiting on the phone.

I said, "I guess I won't see you till school starts?" and he said, "Bumbershoot maybe?" and I said, "Yeah, Bumbershoot." He had a funny look on his face, guilt maybe?

Thank-you-for-the-rides ensued, then it was over. I had felt so uncomfortable. I felt that tight feeling in my throat, like I wanted to cry. I could tell he was uncomfortable too. Maybe it wasn't how he'd wanted it to be either. So then WHY had he decided to make a phone call while we were driving?? Why ruin the nice moment we were having, or why not at least hang up when it was time to say bye, or wait five more minutes to call Sam until after I was gone??

I got out of the car and walked down the driveway to the house. The rain was falling harder now, and I could hear it rustling and plinking on the leaves of the trees. I cried, hoping that Mom wasn't waiting up for me. I just wanted to go to bed, which is where I am now.

And I leave tomorrow. And I don't want to go. I want to go be backstage with Owen forever.

Now he and the rest of the cast are all going to keep hanging out, when the comradery is so fresh after our play just ended. They'll all go to Jenna's party next weekend. Not that Mom and Dad would have let me go even if I WAS going to be in town. But at least it would have felt like an option. He'll probably hook up with someone. Jenna or Annie or Mari or some other cool girl I don't know.

At least we exchanged numbers, and we drove around, and that's better than nothing. Because it WAS. It was something. I have to believe it was. When I woke up, there was his name and number inside my phone. So at least I know it wasn't a dream.

MONDAY, JULY 31, 10:21 A.M.

I'm in the car, driving with Mom and Dad toward Eastern Washington.

It's so cliché, but now I feel hollow. Empty. Now that the play is over, I know that I'm just going to go back to the same monotonous droning of daily life. Pissing off Mom and Dad, getting pissed off by Roxie. No friends, no Owen...yes Owen. I need to be more positive. I'm going to try as hard as I can to get Owen, without trying TOO hard, if you know what I mean.

Roxie isn't coming on the trip after all, which is going to make it 23,000 times more insufferable being only with Mom and Dad. I guess she's too cool now. I wish I would have known it was an option not to go....But Mom and Dad would probably say it's only optional if you're 19.

I miss Owen. Little things about him keep popping into my head. Like how he's the first boy I've ever met who's seen as many old movies as I have. I think it's because he's a dancer (*An American in Paris* is his favorite). We always talked about music and dreamed up extravagant ideas for garden parties and grand balls. I can't stop thinking about that night he drove me home, and the smell of the rain on the asphalt and the way it felt like all the puzzle pieces were falling into place for a kiss, or some kind of romantic goodbye...and of how he ruined it by calling Sam.

I'm worried that I'm forgetting what he looks like.

We just went over the mountain pass and the landscape is starting to look drier and more golden red. Mom wants to stop for peaches near Wenatchee. She and Dad are singing the Woody Guthrie song about the Grand Coulee Dam.

I don't answer. I do, I remember it. And I don't care. I only care about Owen. Has he ever been to the Grand Coulee Dam? I can't believe a week ago we hadn't even started the final shows yet. A week ago, I wasn't even in love with him, was I? I still cared about David then, although that feels like a hundred years ago.

12:23 P.M.

I just had a thought: What if Owen realized mid-car-ride that he was giving off signals that he liked me, by teaching me pool and offering me a ride and asking for my number...but he really didn't and so he panicked and did something utterly unromantic (called Sam) to try to make up for it? Maybe he knew it would ruin the moment and that was the point?

9:10 P.M.

At our first campsite. We originally had set up at one across the highway, but then Mom realized there were nicer, shadier open spots at this site, so while Mom drove the van Dad picked up the entire already-pitched

tent and ran across the road carrying it over his head. I nearly peed laughing. He looked like such a dork! It's pretty here and smells amazing, that sunbaked pine needle scent that always reminds me of summer camping and visiting Mom's parents in California when I was little. Camping with Mom and Dad is mostly boring but kind of nice sometimes.

WE'VE BEEN EATING ALL OUR
TRADITIONAL CAMP FOODS

- KRAFT MACARONI & CHEESE

(WHICH MOM ONLY PERMITS WHILE CAMPING) WITH HOT DOGS CUT IN PENNIES (IN CLASSIC BLUE SPECKLY METAL DISHWARE, OF COURSE.)

- KIPPER SNACKS

(CANNED SMOKED FISH)

- TRAIL MIX (OR GORP, AS MOM CALLS IT.)

- CHEESE PUFFS

GOOD OLD RAISINS & PEANUTS!

- QUAKER INSTANT OATMEAL

(APPLES & CINNAMON FLAVOR ONLY)

- TANG

- LANDJAEGERS

After dinner Dad asked me if I wanted to make Nutkins, the little dolls we'd make out of hazelnuts and moss and sticks on camping trips when I was a kid.

50

I said no and was annoyed. I feel like he still thinks I'm FIVE. A part of me did want to make them, though....I wish Roxie was here. I'm sitting by the fire now trying not to get bit by mosquitoes and failing.

Every time I see a boy at the campsite, I imagine it's Owen. Like what if his family just HAPPENED to be camping at the same site in wherever-the-fuck Eastern Washington? It is nice here...but I want to be home.

TUESDAY, AUGUST 1, 11:48 P.M.

I'm in the tent and I can't sleep, so I'm writing with a headlamp that I hope won't wake up Mom and Dad. We're at a different campsite now. Mom and Dad are driving me WILD. I just want some time to be alone, which is impossible when we're all driving in the same car and doing the same things and staying in the same tent. It's like they don't even know me at all.

I keep thinking of everyone in the play and how close I felt with all of them.

Once at the beginning of *Thoreau* rehearsals, Hanley had us play a game called "If You Really Knew Me."

You just have to start a sentence with "If you really knew me…" and then talk about who you are.

Ms. Hanley said it was important that we all learn to cry and laugh and be vulnerable with each other. It was awkward in the beginning, so she went first.

I was surprised that Mari felt that way. I spend so much time wishing my body looked like hers, I'd never considered that she might be insecure too. Hearing her talk kind of made me miss being real friends, like we were when we were kids. But I doubt she'll keep talking to me now that the summer play is over. Probably when we're back at school she'll pretend she doesn't know me again, like she has for the last few years.

Everyone was so honest about what they were feeling, but I don't know if I was. I didn't say much. I talked a little bit about art, and my family. I still felt so nervous then, intimidated by everyone and just taking in what they were saying. Worried what I would say wouldn't be good enough or would be TOO real and everyone would be uncomfortable. I wish I would have said more, so I'm going to write it here.

IF you REALLY KNEW ME... you'd know I fall in love easily. And that makes me vulnerable, which I don't always like.

IF you REALLY KNEW ME... you'd know I'm afraid of becoming my mother. Because some things I do are the things she does, and I don't like that, because the things she does drive me nuts. She is exactly like her mother, who she hated, and I don't want to be like that. I want to be my own person; I want to find my own way.

IF you REALLY KNEW ME... you'd know that I love my sister more than anyone else. She has been the person I'm most influenced by. My confidant and overall best friend.

IF you REALLY KNEW ME... you'd know I spend most of my time escaping to other worlds, into my head, anywhere that I'm not. You would know that when I see a blank, white wall, my brain paints it with trees and flowers and shapes. Or white turns into clouds, or snow, or the white of the T-shirt Owen always wears....

IF YOU REALLY KNEW ME... you'd know when I'm sad, or happy, when everything builds up inside, I create. I sit down and I paint, or write for hours on end. I cry, and laugh, and try to channel all my feelings through my hands into the things I make.

IF YOU REALLY KNEW ME... you would know that I'm in love and being away from the person I love is one of the hardest things I've ever had to do.

IF YOU REALLY KNEW ME... you'd know I'm insecure. That I want people to remind me that I'm lovable a lot. That sometimes I look in the mirror and try to wish my fat away. The cellulite and stretch marks that I feel like no one else my age even has. That once I squeezed my stomach so hard that my fingers left red welts on my skin. Like if I

squeezed hard enough the fat would just come off, and I'd be free. Free of always feeling like I've failed, of feeling different than everyone else I know. Some days I wish I didn't have a body at all. Not like I want to be dead, but like...I want to just not think about it. Like I want to just BE my mind. BE the stories I tell and things I create instead of having to worry all the time what people think.

WEDNESDAY, AUGUST 2, 11:48 A.M.

We drove through Idaho today. I've never been to Idaho; we're only just passing through the skinny part of it briefly. "Near where they filmed *Smoke Signals*," Mom says. I pretend I don't remember the movie she's talking about even though I do, and I liked it.

2:45 P.M.

Dad won't stop playing the same Bob Dylan tribute CD over and OVER.

Saturday, August 5, 11:31 p.m.

It's been almost a week since I left, which is hard to believe. It feels like it's been a thousand years. To think exactly seven days ago I was in the car with Owen, it's surreal!!! I feel bad because whenever I write, it's about Owen and home. Nothing about the trip.

We arrived in Arlee, Montana, today and have been staying at Mom's college boyfriend Cedar Bob's. His name really is just Cedar but when Mom dated him it was Bob, so she calls him Cedar Bob. Cedar Bob and his wife Windy's farm is in the middle of a vast expanse of field.

Everything in their house is old-fashioned. It's like being in a dollhouse, or one of the life-size dioramas at a museum about pioneers, except more hippieish. Mom and Dad are in the guest room, and I'm tucked in the attic on a little futon with a dusty, ancient patchwork quilt. Right now there is a thunderstorm raging. The roof is metal, and I've never heard rain sound as loud as it does above me now. It's a good thing I'm not tired because it definitely would be hard to sleep. The thunder feels like it's shaking the house, like it's shaking my body from the inside out.

For a split second at a time lightning illuminates the whole entire massive sky and everything looks so blown-out bright and clear.

11:55 P.M.

I just had to pee, and so I crept down the creaky stairs and had to go out into the wild storm to the outhouse! I was too scared to go all the way to the outhouse, though, and ended up just squatting in the field. The cows nearby were mooing, making a racket because of the storm, and I felt so exhilarated running through the rain and lightning cracks! Like I was in a dramatic old movie or something. I'm back in my bed now, and the rain only got me a little bit damp. I love the feeling of going outside in pajamas and peeing freely in the night air.

I wonder what it would be like to kiss Owen in the rain.

Tonight was the night of Jenna's party. So I know he's probably still awake right now, partying with everyone else from the show. Probably rekindling his ol' fling with Jenna, 'cause why not? I just have this sinking feeling like that party was the culmination of the whole summer play and will be what determines who's in the drama in-crowd friend group in the fall. And because I'm not there...I'll just...be forgotten. Maybe someday, in like 15 years, they'll all still be friends and say, "Oh, what ever happened to that Phoebe girl who was only in one play?"

A one-play wonder. Whose most thrilling summer experience thus far has been peeing in the rain.

Sunday, August 6, 10:50 p.m.

We just got back from a party down the road from Cedar Bob and Windy's farm.

At first, I thought it was going to be boring because I was the only person under 50, but then I realized I could just wander around and no one would care, so I went in the house and got myself a Hansen's soda and just started roaming the property, watching drunk old people who all looked like Neil Young reminisce about the 70s.

In the barn there was actually a group of girls my age, all sitting on hay bales and rusty old farm equipment. They had snuck beers and I was a little intimidated by them at first but decided—fuck it. I'll never see these people again. Maybe they'll think I'm some out-of-town loser, but I may as well just be confident and TRY to hang out with them because it's better than not.

LIZZY   TEJA   SIERRA

BEER

ME ACTING AS IF I'VE DEFINITELY DRUNK BEFORE.

I tried to sip my beer like I do it all the time. It was bitter and gross, but I kept drinking it anyway because all of them seemed to be enjoying theirs and I didn't want to be the odd one out. I was afraid that Mom would see me, though, and think I'm an alcoholic. All their parents were also at the party (turns out it was Teja's house) but none of them seemed worried about getting caught drinking. They even carried the beers around when we walked around the party.

A few hours into the party and it was like we had been friends for weeks. I told them all about Owen, and they told me about their various crushes. Sierra had a crush on a boy who was 19! All of them have done a lot of impressive things.

LAST SUMMER AT A RED HOT CHILI PEPPERS CONCERT I WENT UP ON STAGE AND ANTHONY KIEDIS MADE OUT WITH ME.

AND SIERRA HAS BEEN FINGERED BEFORE BY A BOY AT HER SCHOOL.

WOW.

I ended up stretching the truth a little bit about some things I'd done because I was so intimidated by their stories....I know I shouldn't have, but I guess I'll never see them again, so it doesn't REALLY matter.... Maybe I have a serious problem. Mom would probably diagnose me as some kind of pathological liar. I feel bad, because all I'm doing is trying to impress people, even though I know they'd like me just as well if I hadn't lied...maybe. I want Roxie. I want to cry and tell her everything.

When it got late, we went up to Teja's room, which was really cool. Sierra suggested we play the Ouija board and it TOTALLY WORKED. (If you're into that.)

NOTABLE THINGS THE OUIJA SAID

- OWEN IS MY TRUE LOVE
- I AM OWEN'S TRUE LOVE
- WE WILL GO ON A DATE
- I WILL LOSE MY VIRGINITY TO HIM NEXT YEAR, AT A MUSIC FESTIVAL (!!!!)

MONDAY, AUGUST 7, 9:26 P.M.

I am getting SO bored sitting around while Mom and Dad and Windy and Cedar Bob wax on and on about their backcountry trail-building days and play Scrabble by candlelight every night.

I talked to Roxie earlier today on Cedar Bob and Windy's landline after she got off work, and she said her friend's little sister does ballet with Owen. And that she feeds his cat when he's out of town.

I don't know who this bitch is, but I hate her.

LIES I TOLD LAST NIGHT:

- I lied to Roxie about Owen's phone call. I told her that it was Sam who called Owen, and ruined our drive, not the other way around....Lie rating: bad, because it was Roxie.

- I lied to Lizzy, Teja, and Sierra by saying I've been to frat parties with Roxie and taken Jolly Rancher shots. I've actually only just heard about them.

- I also made it seem like I'd drank and smoked pot before.

- I said my first kiss was with my neighbor in his basement.

- I said that when I'm stoned I get really hungry.

- I said I have been "wasted" before.

- I made it seem like the ride home Owen gave me was a "date."

WEDNESDAY, AUGUST 9, 10:25 P.M.

We left Cedar Bob and Windy's house this morning and are at a hotel in Missoula now. I signed on to my Myspace on one of the computers in the hotel lobby and sent Owen a message. He hasn't written anything because it says he hasn't been online.

Last night, Mom and Cedar Bob were looking through old photos from college reminiscing while Dad and Windy were cleaning up after dinner. There were even a few photos of them skinny-dipping with friends in a mountain lake. It was so weird to see pictures of them naked. It made me remember that they were young and wild once too, and it was so strange to think about how Mom had once been with someone who isn't Dad.

Mom was so thin and tan in the pictures. Sometimes I don't even know how I'm her daughter. We look so different, both then and now. When I see old pictures of Mom, I think: Is that what I would look like if I was thin? Is that how I'm SUPPOSED to look, but somehow, somewhere, I took some wrong turn?

Maybe someday I'll get to skinny-dip with Owen.

I've heard that it happens sometimes at Jenna's parties late at night. I might be too insecure, though. Maybe if it was totally dark. I'd be worried that if we were in a group, he'd look at my body and compare it to all the other girls'.

I'm tired, very tired. And getting sick, I think.

THURSDAY, AUGUST 10, 9:46 A.M.

Packing up to leave the hotel. I have a cold.

Twelve days since I last saw Owen. I keep trying to completely re-live that night, remember everything. What if I went outside and Owen was there? What if I went to the lobby and the person at the desk said, "Phoebe, you have a letter," and I looked, and it was from Owen?

What if he has forgotten about me? What if I get home and find out he's with Jenna or Mari or some other girl? Or what if he told his friends he liked me, and they talked him out of it? What if he's thinking the exact same things I am, right now? What if we fall in love? What if we don't?

Teja said Owen and I will hook up at Bumbershoot. I don't think we will, because things like that don't happen to me, and she only thinks they do because of all the lies I've told. I think about them happening, and wish they'd happen, but they never do. But it almost did…then he called Sam. Was he scared?

I think maybe there is no meaning of life. I think people are born, and they eat, shit, fight, fuck, and die. Maybe that's it. Maybe it's ridiculous to worry about not-received Myspace messages. Maybe I should go out and do what life is really about, eating, fucking, and dying. I kind of want to have sex with Owen. I want to have a baby and a garden and an old house with sunflowers before we all die from global warming.

SATURDAY, AUGUST 12, 1:23 P.M.

I'm dying. My nose is going to internally combust from stuffiness.

We are almost HOME. I am so ready for this trip to be over. It wasn't as bad as I thought it was going to be with only Mom and Dad, but I'm DONE. I have suffered through many a silent meal. And almost worse than the silence is the small talk, the thinly veiled attempts to "draw me out of my shell" by talking about things they think I'm interested in. It's like I'm drowning in a sea of petty conversation and arguments that have no purpose but to aggravate me to my deepest core.

Most of the time they treat me like some inferior small child or tiny dog.

"PHOEBE," they reprimanded me once, upon me confiscating a prawn from my dad's plate (that he was done with, by the way!!!).

It makes me want to eat more just to make him mad.

I am tired of being in the car with them. I miss Roxie. Though I'd probably be annoyed with her too if she was here.

When I get home I want to do something risky. I'm tired of living the same mundane day over and over again. I want to go and get drunk and dance and run and scream. I will hook up with Owen. Even if it takes some liquid confidence to do so.

Monday, August 14, 12:15 a.m.

I'm home. I have been for two days. It's weird being back, at least it was at first, but now I'm getting used to it. It was nice seeing Roxie. I forgot what it feels like to be around someone who knows everything about you and you know everything about them.

I was on Myspace and saw that Owen has signed on, but he hasn't replied to my message yet. Roxie says I shouldn't care.

She says I shouldn't let myself get myself too wrapped up in him because I don't REALLY know him. But I do know him....At least I think I do. Or thought I did. OKAY, I don't. But she wasn't there. She can't shut her eyes and remember his smile, his smell, his hands and face, what it felt like to hug him and stand next to him and drive with him and talk with him. Do I really feel differently about him than any other asshole I've liked? Is he just another asshole? What if I never see him again??

I should try to be less excited about him, because he'll never be as great as I've built him up in my head. I've made him into some perfect person, a dreamy, freckly ballerina boy who I already get along with perfectly. But when I look back on it, for the most part, it's probably all been a lie.

I think I lied to Roxie about it being Sam who called Owen while we were driving, not the other way around, because I wanted to convince myself that that was true. That it was out of his hands in some way. Even when I'm being honest about him making the call, I keep defending him, telling myself that it wasn't THAT ass-y of a thing to do...and maybe it wasn't. Maybe I totally overreacted, and a cooler, less needy girl wouldn't care that he called his friend and didn't give a perfect goodbye.

In 20 years, I'll look back and laugh over this journal, filled with the ranting and raving about the awkwardness of high school. But although I can see past all of this, I still find it hard to believe this isn't important or at all relevant to my life in the future. Maybe I'll hook up with Owen and we'll date and he'll be my first love, and this will be a special memento to where it all began. But maybe not. Maybe he'll move to

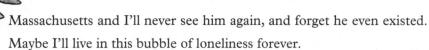

Massachusetts and I'll never see him again, and forget he even existed. Maybe I'll live in this bubble of loneliness forever.

I biked downtown with Roxie today to get bagels and

bought a pair of cute boots at the cool hipster store, and new CDs.

I saw Jenna and Sam at Haggen's market, and they said they'd been hanging out with Owen and Lukas at the lake. But I don't care. I'm trying to care less. Or at least seem like I care less.

Sam cut off all his hair and is looking less clown-ular, though his style still needs improvement. He was wearing some wack sporty wraparound sunglasses that I wanted to chuck into the fires of Mount Doom.

I'm worried, because I worry about everything. There's just so much to think about. I can feel fall in the air—the wind is whistling outside. Which means school is starting soon. There's West Nile virus, flesh-eating bacteria, laundry…global warming. I need a new toothbrush, and Mom is always hounding me to exercise more. I should really take more black-and-white photos, or get a Polaroid, and get better about drawing in my sketchbook. My room is messy, autumn is coming…and then there's Owen.…So much on my mind and more. I'm going to sleep now.

FRIDAY, AUGUST 18, 9:46 p.m.

I hung out with Nora today for the first time outside the play.

I took the bus downtown and met her at Fiamma Burger. I asked Mom if I could use her bus pass that she has through work, but she said no!!!

She is such a stickler sometimes that it just makes me want to SCREAM and rebel in some extreme way.

So anyway, I had to pay the $1 fare. Nora and I mostly just talked about what classes we were taking, and what play we thought Ms. Hanley was gonna pick for the fall show, and who would get the leads, etc. When we were finished eating, we walked around with our milkshakes and window-shopped. I told her about how Mari and I were friends when we were kids, but how now I'm intimidated by Mari and Jenna because they're all so beautiful and perfect.

She said yes, everyone was different, some nerdier and some more popular (like Lukas, Mari, and Jenna), some shy (like her), and some more wild (like Annie), but that those differences felt like a part of what made shows and hanging out so fun. "The plays are different during school. *Thoreau* was fun but it felt more...scattered because of the summertime. Just wait, you'll see what it's like. Everyone gets so close, it's simply divine."

I asked her if she went to any of Jenna's wild parties last year or during the summer. She said she was at a cast party at Jenna's that got rowdy, where people were drinking. She said, "Everyone just acted really silly and annoying so I went home."

I kind of nodded. It felt like there wasn't any room for me to be curious and want to do that stuff. Like she wouldn't approve.

Saturday, August 19, 11:35 p.m.

I saw David Berglund today. Roxie and I were walking past Haggen's and he drove by. He smiled, etc., and I did too.

I forgot how cute he is, but I don't think I really like him anymore, which is okay because if he ever liked me at some point, I highly doubt he still does, when he has an endless number of girls at his disposal.

There was an outdoor movie tonight. I walked down there and silently mocked the newly graduated eighth graders hanging out with their posses on the corners.

I acted like a bitch. I stared at them like I knew I was better than them. In their Hollister tank tops and jean shorts, their hair straightened to crisps, they all looked the same, McMannequins.

I don't care if they think I'm a cold, hard bitch. At least I have integrity.

Before I left the house, I'd snuck some of Mom's raspberry liqueur that she uses for cooking and poured it into a water bottle. Mom and Dad never drink any of the stuff in the cabinet where all the liquor is kept, and I bet they won't EVER notice that some of the alcohol she uses like once every two years is gone.

I drank just enough of it to feel a warmth spread over my whole body and make me feel just a little bit giggly and confident. But of course I didn't see anyone I actually cared about, just kids younger than me and a few familiar faces from my grade.

I went over to Nora's today for the first time. She has a huge yard that backs up to the woods, and we wandered around taking glamour photos of us against mossy rocks and stuff.

Nora is very into Star Wars, and she was deeply scandalized when I told her I haven't seen the original three, and said we had to have a movie night soon. She has seen so many movies, and quotes them in accents all the time out of the blue. I wish I read as much as her—I read a lot but she does like two books a week and has read the whole Silmarillion, and Star Wars Expanded Universe. Not His Dark Materials, though, which I said I'd loan her because she simply MUST. She said she would teach me to French braid my hair, which I don't know how to do. She does everyone's hair for the plays because she's so good.

Friday, September 1, 7 p.m.

School starts next week!

And I think I don't like Owen anymore. Maybe. I don't know.

Today was registration and picture day for school. I saw Mari and Lukas and Jenna, and they all waved and were friendly, rather than shunning me like I'd feared! Phew.

I didn't see Owen until I was leaving. He was driving away with Annie in her car. But the strange thing was, when I saw him, I didn't feel anything. No skipping heart, or even excitement. It was just Owen. That's it. I think I'm over him! Maybe I'll see him at Bumbershoot this weekend, maybe I won't. Maybe I'll hook up with him, like the Ouija board predicted...but probably I won't.

If I see him when I'm with Roxie, she'll probably say something cold or dismissive because she's protective and thinks he's annoying. We're going to be staying overnight in one of her friends' apartments in the U District. I am SO excited. Roxie and I got Hannah, my math tutor from last year, to buy us some vodka and rum because she's in college and 21. And since Bumbershoot searches your bags at the gate, Roxie is putting it in plastic water bottles and then duct-taping them to her thighs under a loose-fitting dress. I hope it works! I'm so nervous that she'll get caught!

WEDNESDAY, SEPTEMBER 6, ? P.M.

I'm sorry I haven't written in almost a week—everything has been so busy. Mom left Tuesday for a social work conference in Nashville. Which means Roxie and I are stuck with Dad's experimental cooking. There's already been many a brown rice and vegetable stir-fry dusted with nutritional yeast and complete with slimy foraged mushrooms.

I FOUND THEM OUTSIDE MY OFFICE... DON'T WORRY, THEY'RE NOT THE PSYCHEDELIC KIND!

Bumbershoot was SO fun and overwhelming and tiring but amazing. I got "real" drunk for the first time and acted très ridicule, but luckily no one who I cared about embarrassing myself in front of was there. We saw Blue Scholars and Of Montreal, Metric, Feist, Rogue Wave, and a bunch of other random bands.

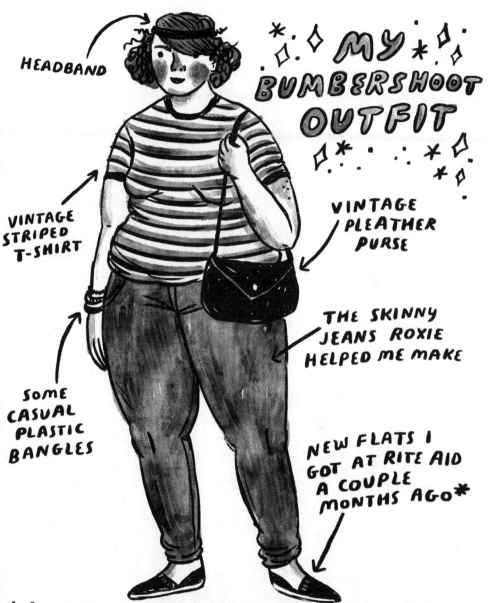

HEADBAND

*.◇ ◇ ・ *・◇ *・
MY
BUMBERSHOOT
OUTFIT
◇・* ・ ・* ◇◇

VINTAGE
STRIPED
T-SHIRT

VINTAGE
PLEATHER
PURSE

THE SKINNY
JEANS ROXIE
HELPED ME MAKE

SOME
CASUAL
PLASTIC
BANGLES

NEW FLATS I
GOT AT RITE AID
A COUPLE
MONTHS AGO*

*(ALL THE HIPSTERS ARE WEARING THEM. THEY
ARE CUTE BUT ARE BASICALLY PIECES OF NOTHING,
AND AFTER WALKING AROUND ALL DAY IT FELT
LIKE MY FEET WERE JUST PULVERIZED MEAT PADS
BEING SLAMMED REPEATEDLY INTO THE HARD GROUND.)

On top of that, I got my period, super heavy, and had to walk around all day sweating with a giant shitty, chafe-y pad that I had to get last minute from the bathroom dispenser that felt like a chunky plastic diaper. It actually makes me glad that I DIDN'T see Owen, which I never thought I'd say. I kept having to ask Roxie all night if there was blood coming through my

jeans. Being drunk was so weird, like having a fever or something! Everything was such a blur. I didn't get sick, though, thank goodness. We slept on the carpeted floor at the apartment of one of Roxie's friends who goes to UW, which was not comfortable at all. Luckily, I was so tired and drunk that I didn't notice until morning.

Mom does NOT know that we drank and that Hannah bought us any alcohol; she CANNOT find out. Roxie says Mom thinks anyone who drinks anything is an alcoholic because her mom was one and so she's ultra conservative about drinking.

Which is true. She always kind of SNIFFS when family friends even bring wine or beer over during a potluck, and last year when I wanted to buy an Iron & Wine T-shirt, she wouldn't let me because she said it was "promoting alcohol" even though it's just the name of a BAND!

I STILL WISH I HAD IT

Friday, September 8, 9:55 p.m.

School started! OFFICIALLY a sophomore! It's OKAY. So far. I am still technically a homeschooler, which means I get to take only the fun classes and not worry about graduation requirements, which is nice. I have French 3, then Drama 3 (I should be in Drama 2, but Ms. Hanley let me skip because I did the play), then Yearbook last. I was surprised at how many people I knew in drama class: Mari, Jenna, Nora, Annie, Lukas, Sam, and of course David Berglund. No Owen, though. He must be taking a different elective. I had thought they all would have taken Drama 3 already, but they said because there is no drama class above level 3, everyone just repeats it over and over so they can hang out and get practice.

Asher Wilson is in my Yearbook class again. He was in it last year too and was basically the only person who talked to me, when I was a freshman and didn't know anyone. He would always come up to me when I was doodling in class and ask about my art. Then we started talking about indie music and joking around. He's one of the only other people at school I know who wears vintage clothes and listens to all the same bands I do. He's also always referencing bands I haven't heard of, and sometimes tells me bands he thinks I'd like to look up on Myspace.

ASHER WILSON

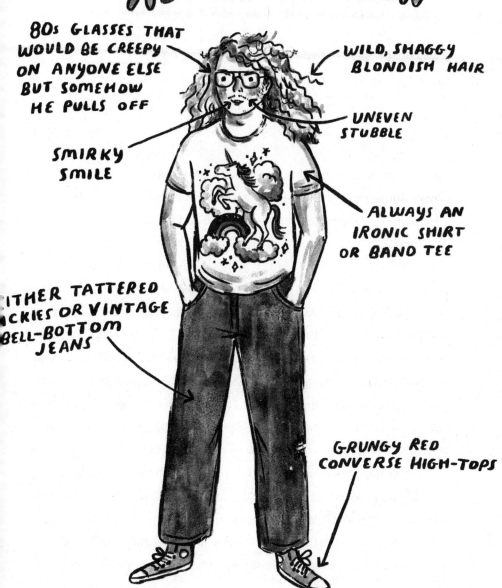

80s GLASSES THAT WOULD BE CREEPY ON ANYONE ELSE BUT SOMEHOW HE PULLS OFF

WILD, SHAGGY BLONDISH HAIR

UNEVEN STUBBLE

SMIRKY SMILE

ALWAYS AN IRONIC SHIRT OR BAND TEE

ITHER TATTERED CKIES OR VINTAGE BELL-BOTTOM JEANS

GRUNGY RED CONVERSE HIGH-TOPS

When I came into class, he said "Hey" with a smirky smile like he just knew I was happy to see him, which I was. I said "Hey" and we hung out the rest of class. Last year he would give me rides home sometimes (even though he technically wasn't allowed to because he only had his permit) and I would make fun of him for driving a different Subaru to school every day. I said, "Why do you have a fleet of Subarus?" and he said, "We only have two! An old one and a new one." But now it's our running joke. Anyway. He has his license now. I can't tell if he thinks I'm cool or an obnoxious baby. He only has a few people at our school he hangs out with, seniors mostly (he's a junior). Last year I had a crush on one of his friends, Dylan, and was always wishing he would invite me to hang out or eat lunch with them, but he never did. Probably because he was embarrassed to hang out with me outside of Yearbook class.

I think we are friends, but not like real friends because we don't talk much outside of class, or about our feelings or things in our life very much. Which is kind of just how boys are in general, I guess.

The best part of school so far has just been hanging out with everyone at lunch. It's right before drama, so we all hang out in the courtyard outside the Little Theater and eat and talk. Mari, Annie, and Lukas are seniors, so they left campus for lunch one day since they're allowed, but it was still so fun just with Nora, Sam, Jenna, and me. Sam has a really funny, dry, snarky sense of humor and is always rolling his eyes at whatever goofy, fanciful tangent Nora and I are on. He was also scandalized that I'd never seen Star Wars and agreed with Nora that a movie night was in order ASAP. I tried to explain that I HAVE seen at least one of the newer ones, in theaters when it came out. "Which ones?" Sam asked suddenly, with a very serious look on his face. "There was, like, racing

94

around in a desert and a tall salamander guy," I said, and Sam and Nora just shook their heads. "This is dire. A movie night is in order. Or maybe a series of movie nights," Sam said, and then in a Yoda voice, "Much work ahead of us, there is," and Nora said, teasing, "That's how Yoda talks—do you know who Yoda is?"

Roxie and I were at Trek Video earlier and who should walk in but David Berglund. It was so surreal because it was one of those things I always imagine happening every time I go somewhere, but never actually does. One minute I'd been talking about him, and then he was there, talking on his cell phone. My heart was beating so fast I thought I was going into cardiac arrest.

Sometimes I still suspect he likes me. Now that we're back in drama together, it's funny, we have this strange connection. I find myself avoiding eye contact, because if we do make eye contact it holds for a long time and it's like I'm sinking into him and won't be able to get out. Today we were all sitting onstage in a circle, and he was across from me and we stared at each other, and I felt vulnerable, as if by looking at my eyes he could read my mind and know my feelings for him, which, by the way, I don't know what they are.

DO I LIKE HIM AGAIN ???

Saturday, September 9, 1:50 p.m.

On the boy front, nothing much has happened except during drama class David asked me if I got any good movies at Trek. I said, "*Six Feet Under*...the show," and he said, "Oh, is that good?" and I said, "Yes." Then I asked him and he said he got *Rent* and some French movie. Of course, he's so sophisticated. And that was it.

I shouldn't like him. I know the only real reason I do is because he gives me attention. However miniscule, it's attention. And I'm not getting any from anyone else right now, so I'm bored.

During *Thoreau* I liked David, then Owen started paying more attention to me, so I liked him more. I don't really know either of them, and spending hours looking at their Myspaces (like I did last night) doesn't help.

I sat across from David in our circle onstage during class again to test if the funny energy was between us today, or if it's all in my head. I tried not to sense anything. I tried to realize that maybe there was nothing between us, no special force-tastic energy. But my brain couldn't let go of the hope that it wasn't just NOTHING.

The life I lead is in my head. The witty conversations I have, the first kiss and dates and losing of virginity, the hookups, breakups, children, husbands, outfits, they're all in my head. I've never really liked any boy for who they were, just the idea of them. I want to REALLY get to know someone, not just another character in my stories. I'm tired of living in my stories. And I think that's all I've ever done. Owen. David. It's all fiction. In my head I can be anyone. I can be someone worthy of their attention.

SUNDAY, SEPTEMBER 10, 3:19 P.M.

Sitting at the fucking shitty hairdresser's in Sunset Square while Roxie gets a cheap haircut and blond dye job. Everyone in here is wearing chunky shoes. Thinking about David, hoping to see him, knowing I'm not going to.

Tuesday, September 12, 9:55 p.m.

Auditions for the fall play, *Tom Jones*, were today! I was super, super nervous and thought I did really badly, but my group (Lukas, David, Mari, and Nora) told me I was good. I saw Owen. Of course. I knew I would. All the people auditioning were sitting in the Little Theater, and he smiled and mouthed "Hi" and so did I. Later he came over and asked how my audition went and I said, "Okay." Then I asked how he was, and he said good. And that was it.

After auditions I walked with Nora and Annie and David to get coffee at Tony's. Up until then, I had been thinking that David was still acting like he liked me. Grabbing my attention and looking at me and such. But it was when we were all at Tony's drinking our coffees (well, tea for me) and eating fudge, listening to David talk about all the girls he's made out with, etc., etc., and his "kind of" girlfriend, who he had sex with last year, that I realized he doesn't like me at all. Well, MAYBE he did, for a half a second, or however long he likes any girl, because now I'm realizing David likes everyone.

He was egged on by Annie, of course, who always wants to show everyone how comfortable she is talking about sex and how close she and David are. I could tell Nora was super uncomfortable. I never hear her talk about that kind of stuff. And I kind of was too, but I also wanted to hear it all.

I feel like David tricked me into thinking he's some mountain-man intellectual, but really he's this nice and funny but self-centered player. And I'm not saying that I dislike him and don't want to be his friend. I'm saying that I need to stop falling for any guy who blinks an eye in my general direction. It's unhealthy. But…I know I won't be able to just STOP. Because it's not that easy. And because I'm lonely. So lonely.

I'm très ridicule, I know. Good night.

WEDNESDAY, SEPTEMBER 13, 9:50 P.M.

Callbacks for the play were today. I made them!!

During Yearbook class Mrs. Lynn had Asher Wilson and me take photos for the "Students' Fave Spots" page, so we basically got to spend an entire period driving around town taking pictures of the restaurants and places to hang out that students go to most. It turned into Asher and me just taking goofy photos of each other at all the locations.

I like Asher. Not in a crush way. Just in a friends way. Today he said "Cool shirt" about my Death Cab tee and asked if I saw them play at WWU two years ago. I almost lied and said yes but decided not to, and said no. Because it would have been too easy to get caught in the lie. I wasn't cool enough two years ago to have gone to a show. He has good CDs in his car. We listened to Sufjan Stevens, Neutral Milk Hotel, and the Flaming Lips, who I hadn't heard before. He said he'd make me a mix.

After Yearbook class I ran to the theater for callbacks, where David was hanging around acting irresistible. He made callbacks too, of course, because he's brilliant, as did all the regulars. I auditioned for all my roles I wanted but I thought I did shitty.

11:10 P.M.

Sorry, I was called upon by Roxie to watch *Six Feet Under*. Anyway. Throughout auditions I felt horrible, really nervous, and then after I went, I felt like shit and was beating myself up inside while being all happy-go-lucky Phoebe on the outside. It seemed as if everyone except me had everything going for them. No one told me I did good, so I assumed it was awful. It wasn't until I was home, in my room, and David called me that I felt better. Yes. David called ME. This confirms that perhaps I'm NOT a blithering fool or a silent, mouselike ghost around him.

Then he said something along the lines of "Au contraire," and we proceeded to play the "You were so good," "No, you were so good" game until it was a small silence that was mostly his phone having bad reception. After that it was idle chitchat for about a minute longer. Then it was over.

I'm surprised I wasn't more surprised or excited that he called me??? Tomorrow the list of who got parts will be posted. I honest to god have no idea what part I'll get. I'm only about 50% sure I'll even GET a part. Mrs. Western and Lady Bellaston are the two older-lady character parts, which Nora and I are most likely get because we are not "leading lady" types (i.e., thin with big boobs). I hope I don't get Mrs. Whitefield, the barkeep, because I at least want to wear a pretty dress!

Sunday, September 17, 9:27 p.m.

I got cast in the play!!! I was so relieved when I saw my name on the list on Thursday.

I got the part of Mrs. Western!!!!

Monday, September 18, 7:55 p.m.

Today was the first read-through of the script! It went well. I have quite a few lines and the play is très, très funny. When I started reading my character, I for some reason adopted this haughty, rich British woman voice that gets weirdly asthmatic and high and everyone went wild laughing whenever I talked. I determined that Mrs. Western talks like this because of the years she spent in tight corsets that restricted her breathing. Sam made his role, who's my character's brother, into a big character too, doing a gruff, blustering country gentleman–type British accent.

The two of us were bouncing off each other and making people crack up so hard, and it felt so good to make people laugh, because I feel like I was such a shy, introverted mouse during the summer play because I was so intimidated by everyone. But all of a sudden, through my character, I was able to express the wilder, more funny side of myself.

In other news, we finished the second season of *Lost* on DVD. The show to which my whole family is shamelessly addicted.

And Roxie left today for Seattle. She had been home for summer, before her new lease started. We all drove her down in the van and helped move her into her new apartment in the U District, near the  Ave (which has so many cool thrift stores plus the Sanrio store and tons of good food).

I've already called her twice. I both miss her and am a little bit glad she's gone....I'm looking forward to coming home to an empty house after school every day. I kind of love being home alone and getting to do whatever I want in the quiet. Plus, her leaving means I get to go visit. The weather here is starting to be more on the cold and rainy side. Fall seems to actually be happening this year. I can't wait for the storms in November, when it pours and the wind is so strong it's like the house is being torn apart. And then it will be biting-cold winter, when I can be cozy indoors.

I remember last year, the first year Roxie lived in Seattle. I'd visited her almost every weekend. It was before I really made any friends at school, so going and seeing her was my whole social life. We'd dress up cute and freeze to death as we waited with her friends for a bus to take us from Belltown to the U District, where we ate gyros and sought refuge from the cold inside the vintage store Tiger Tiger on the Ave.

Then we bused back to her house, our fingers numb, and watched figure skating on the Winter Olympics. That was back before Owen and David, before I became a drama kid and hipster and started making real friends. Before *Thoreau* and Montana, when Roxie was still a brunette and I still wore flare jeans. I feel so different now, older. More mature, more confident. Definitely an improvement.

Tuesday, September 19, 9:17 p.m.

I'm at the Mitchells' babysitting Brandon and Ella now. They are easy to babysit because they just want to hyper-ly show me everything they've made lately and do Mad Libs and make me draw pictures.

After that I let them watch some silent French film they're obsessed with 'cause they're not allowed to watch mainstream movies (childhood me can relate).

I just put them to bed, and everything is quiet now. I wish they had cable so I could watch some TV. All there is to do is write on their rock-hard futon. Sometimes the parents of kids I babysit tell me to help myself to snacks or give me dinner, but the Mitchells never do, and I'm STARVING.

They have some kind of honey-soaked fried pastry in the kitchen under plastic wrap and I keep going and sneaking bits of it every few minutes. I think it's at the point where they'll definitely start noticing

if I keep eating it, though. So, I must. Practice. Self.
Restraint. Which is hard because I'm SO hungry that I
could just about die.

We had our second real play practice today, not just the read-through.
It was lots of fun starting to get into blocking. As I was leaving, Owen
was behind me and he asked if I was getting picked up, and if he could
get a ride. I told him I was walking, and he walked with me. It felt a little
bit like old times, during *Thoreau*. We talked about this and that, then
Bumbershoot. I restrained myself from trying to impress him by telling
him how drunk I was, because I knew I'd feel silly afterward. Even if I
felt temporarily cool, it wouldn't be worth it in the long run.

   We were talking about the Blue Scholars show, and I said something
about how I remember how sweaty the main guy was. Then before I
knew it, Owen started telling me how HE sweats all the time.

It was so extremely awkward, like what are you supposed to say when someone starts talking about their overactive sweat glands?

Should I have told him I have the same problem to make him feel less alone? Then he had to turn left and

I FELT HORRIBLE!!

go to his house, so that's how our hangout ended. Another awkwardly odd parting of ways with Owen McCloud.

How is it that around some people I can be so outgoing and funny, and other times my mind goes completely blank? I feel so ridiculously out of my element trying to carry on a conversation with one other person who I don't know very well. And it's not like I'm afraid to be myself (well, maybe a bit). It's more like I don't really know HOW to be myself. It's like I don't really know WHO I am. How does Phoebe act? Around friends? Around boys? I can't act the same way around Owen that I can around Roxie or Nora, because…it's just different. I talk about different things with each person and have kind of a different language with each person. And I don't know what my language is with boys or half friends like Owen yet.

Maybe I should have comforted Owen, or said I'd never noticed his sweat?

I never know what to say or do. An optimistic take on this could be that Owen feels comfortable enough around me to tell me something like that. Maybe he needed to get it out of the way because he was afraid of me not liking him if I found out on my own. On the other, more likely, hand, he was offended that I would be so judgmental of someone based on his sweatiness and had to lecture me, since I'm such an utterly mean and cruel-hearted person compared to him, whom the saying "Wouldn't hurt a fly" was based on.

And you know what? It pisses me off that Owen "wouldn't hurt a fly" because flies are so fucking annoying that I want to hurt them sometimes. I don't even know if I like Owen anymore. Maybe he's too awkward. I don't think I do. Maybe there's a teeny, miniscule particle of me that still has hope that he's harboring a secret love for me, but mostly I'm over him. If there's one person I'd still like, it would be David. And I don't, not in a serious way, just in a you-are-so-beautiful-and-roguish way. I think the REAL reason I have any inkling of liking for either of them is for lack of anything else.

10:30 P.M.

Back home in bed. Thinking how frustrating it is that all I can do about my problems and crushes is hash and rehash them in this book over and over and over again. Fuck.

I'm gonna listen to my iPod now.

EXCEPT FUCK. THE BATTERY JUST DIED.

And I remembered I'm in mourning because I didn't get the new Ben Kweller CD that came out today, because I'm so fucking busy! Fuck fuck fuck.

THURSDAY, SEPTEMBER 21, 11:09 P.M.

I HATE BEING AN ARTIST.
I HATE EVERYTHING I CREATE.

Every line I draw, the doodles and paintings, puppets, screen prints, block prints, all of it. None of it is original. Every single artistic thought I've sketched onto paper makes me SICK.

It's just some shit imitation of the work of someone more talented than I. Everything has been done before. Are artists just supposed to admit defeat in this day and age? Committing their lives to creating laughable versions of great art? What if I'm not really an artist? What if this very thing that I've always thought is what I want is what will lead to my destruction? I'm being driven wild. I see the art I'm surrounded by and think about how utterly wretched the things I create are. I could never be a famous artist. I could never have my art displayed in tall-ceilinged galleries, with sterile white walls and wood floors. I could never be the proud and deep creator chatting with my red-wine-sipping clients.

I remember when I was little, and I would read books that were biographies of famous artists and writers, and I'd think, "Someday maybe I'll be in there." "Born in Bellingham, Washington, in 1991, died in 20??." It is ridiculous to think about that now. Now there are no famous artists, just movie stars and musicians. With the exception of people like Matthew Barney, you don't become famous if you're an artist these days. I want to stop everything and go do real art, but I don't know how, and I'm so afraid. It fucking pisses me off how afraid I am. Afraid of everything: death, artistic failure, love, intimacy, the theater, art art art art art. Afraid of what people think.

WHY DOES EVERYTHING HAVE TO BE SO DIFFICULT?? WHY CAN'T A PERSON TELL SOMEONE THEY LIKE THEM? WHY COULDN'T I JUST HAVE TOLD OWEN I LIKED HIM THAT NIGHT WHEN HE GAVE ME A RIDE HOME? NOW IT FEELS LIKE OUR ONE CHANCE WAS BLOWN AND IT'S AWKWARD, LIKE THE SPELL OF SUMMER IS BROKEN.

SATURDAY, SEPTEMBER 30, 12:24 P.M.

Last night was the Ben Kweller concert at WWU. It was one of the most amazing nights of my life.

We got there early so we could get right in the front, and we did. I was with Nora, who I've been hanging out with more and more. She isn't into indie music and didn't know who Ben Kweller was but came with me anyway. We saw Owen there too, in line. He gave us a friendly wave—and I barely felt anything. I really do think I'm over him. I barely think about him at all anymore. In fact, I haven't really thought about any of my crushes much lately. A local band called Misty

BK CONCERT OUTFIT

PLASTIC DAISY CLIP

CHUNKY RED BEADS

BLUE-AND-WHITE DRESS THAT ROXIE SEWED ME

HOMEMADE BK BUTTON!!

VINTAGE PINK BELT (I HAD TO POKE A NEW HOLE IN IT TO MAKE IT FIT)

CUTE LEATHER PURSE THAT I "BORROWED" FROM MOM

COOL 80S BOOTS FROM GOODWILL

Mountains opened for him, and guess who the drummer was?? Asher Wilson from my Yearbook class! He looked so cool drumming up onstage, the same stage that BEN KWELLER was going to play on! His long wild hair was shaking all around while he drummed, and he wore cool 70s bell-bottom jeans that buttoned up the front and a turquoise tank top.

After their set there was a break before BK went on, and Asher came over to say hi. His neck was shiny with sweat, and I could smell his BO.

He said "Hey" all casual and I said "Hey" and asked why he didn't tell me he was in a band. He just shrugged and gave me his smirky smile. His eyes kept flicking over to a group of girls who go to our school and were hanging out by his band's merch table. He probably thinks they're cute, and they probably think he's a sex god since he's in a band.

I did feel a little cool talking to him, someone who opened for Ben Kweller. Maybe he didn't want to tell me he was in a band because he didn't want me to come to his shows and embarrass him. I'm proud of myself for having him as a kind of friend. Usually I develop crushes on like every boy I even minorly interact with, so I feel like it's proof I'm maturing that we just hang out in Yearbook and are friends.

Nora thought he was cute and asked if he went to our school. When I said yeah, she said, "I can't believe I've never noticed him before." I didn't tell her that I hang out with him every Yearbook period. I think because I don't want her to come around and try to hang out with us. I like Nora but I don't think she'd "get" someone like Asher. He's not into quoting Monty Python and dressing up in fancy old-time outfits, which is mostly what Nora and I do when we hang out. And I wouldn't want her to get her hopes up because I don't think she's his type. Not that I really know what his type is. Her saying something about Asher was the first time I've even heard her talk about a boy that way. I'm always feeling like the wild, boy-crazy one in our relationship because they're ALL I want to talk about most of time, but she just wants to talk about movies and books and will change the subject when I want to talk about boys and sex and stuff. I don't really get it—I know neither of us has had any experience, but doesn't she think it's at ALL exciting to think about?

Anyway.

Ben Kweller was phenomenal.

I screamed so loud that by the end my voice was cracking like a twelve-year-old boy's. He played things off his new album, and his old ones, and I knew all the words and took TONS of pictures with a slowed-down shutter speed so it looked like the lights were swirling around.

♥♥BEN KWELLER!♥

From where I was standing, I could see Asher offstage. Sarah Sokolowski, who is a senior and was in my French class last year, was with him and the rest of the band. A couple times I made eye contact with him while BK was playing, and we just beamed at each other or made goofy faces. He's really the only other person I know who really gets it, how amazing the show was.

After it was all over, I got a T-shirt. And then WE MET HIM. BEN KWELLER.

He signed my shirt and ticket stub, with a silver Sharpie, and we got pictures with him!!! He even saw my homemade pin I painted!!!!

After talking to BK (no big deal...), Nora and I went back near Asher's band's merch table and I had him sign my ticket stub too. Half jokingly but half for real because his band is really good and you never know, maybe they'll become famous someday! I think he thought I was a total dork. Sarah Sokolowski was still with him and her arm was linked through his. I think maybe they're a couple, but he's never said anything about her to me and I hang out with him almost every day during class.

SARAH SOKOLOWSKI

HIP HAIRCUT →

AMAZING GLASSES. I WISH I NEEDED GLASSES SO I COULD HAVE COOL VINTAGE ONES.

TRÈS COOL INDIFFERENT LOOK →

← BANDANNA

I think Nora noticed that Sarah was with him too because she didn't talk about him again, even though I noticed her cheeks get really red when I introduced her. Asher just said "Hey" to Nora and then started talking to me about one of BK's songs until Sarah tugged on his arm and they walked away.

Sunday, October 1, 10:40 p.m.

Who are we kidding, I'll probably never be in a relationship. Maybe in college or something. I just feel like boys my age are so immature and awkward. COUGH...Owen...COUGH.

Today I started watercoloring loose, black-lined paintings of people. Hipsters mostly with outfits I want to have or who I wish I was friends with. One looked exactly like Asher, so I posted it on his Myspace, and he liked it. He asked if I could bring it to Yearbook tomorrow for him to keep. I decided to move my art from the table in the family

room to the desk in my bedroom because I'm tired of Mom and Dad always coming around and complimenting my work. I hate feeling like I can't make whatever I want because what if they won't like it or think it's inappropriate or weird, I feel like they just want me to make paintings of fruit and owls and stuff forever.

ART LIKE I USED TO MAKE.

Last night I went to Nora's house for a girls' night sleepover and it was really fun. It was Mari, Annie, Jenna, Nora, and me. It was the first time we've really all hung out so intimately, but it wasn't awkward at all and it was surprisingly fun to hang out with Mari outside of drama stuff.

I would have thought she'd be too "cool" for something as little-girly as a sleepover, especially because she's a senior, but she was totally into it. She even referenced sleepovers we'd had as kids with Roxie in front of everyone at one point. It was one of the first times she acknowledged we'd been friends before. Even Annie was less rowdy in such a small group. It seems like she doesn't feel the need to be as wild and loud without boys around.

We stayed up super late talking, mainly about crushes.

Nora kept trying to steer the conversation elsewhere, but no one can get in the way of Annie once she starts gossiping.

I said Owen for mine, even though things have been kind of awkward and nonexistent with him....I didn't want to say David because I knew he'd be Annie's. And he was. She talked all about how they're such good friends, but she feels like he doesn't see her as having romantic potential, that she's often "one of the boys" to guys. I wonder if that's why she is always talking about sex and trying to be so over-the-top flirty.

Mari said she likes Lukas...! She said they've "hooked up" before, last year, and that it always feels like there's tension between them. But that it doesn't seem like he wants to really "date." That he's had plenty of opportunities to ask her to dances and stuff but hasn't.

Jenna said she likes Tim, who wasn't in *Thoreau*, but is in the chorus of *Tom Jones*.

Nora said nobody, to which we all moaned because it was such a letdown and we didn't want the juicy crush content to run out.

"Asher Wilson?" Annie said. "Yeah," I said. "We saw him at the Ben Kweller show. He was in the opening band. He's in my Yearbook class." "He's hot but I've heard he's a certified freak," Annie said. "He comes off all dorky and grungy, but he's slept with, like, thirty girls." "I don't know if I can get past the pervstache," Jenna added.

I could tell this was making Nora uncomfortable, so I tried to change the subject, but Annie kept going. "He's had sex with all the artsy girls and all the band girls, pretty much. I know with Lindsay Duncan and Taylor Wilde, at least. And now he's with that Sarah girl."

"Sarah is cool, though," Jenna chimed in. "She's in my bio class."

I can't stop wondering if all of that is true. It's so weird because I hang out with Asher every day at school, and sometimes outside of school if we have to cover an event together for Yearbook, but I know almost nothing about his personal life. Maybe he IS secretly some wild player, I'd never know, and it's not a thing you just ask a male friend randomly. One thing I know for sure is that if he IS, he's DEFINITELY not a good match for Nora. She's practically allergic to sex.

It's so boring being so woefully crushless at the moment. Owen and David just kind of feel like filler fluff now that my interactions with them have waned. Like they'll always be around, taunting me with their twinkly eyes and adorable smiles, Owen with his freckles and David with his dashing airs....But they just feel stagnant. Like they're caricatures of crushes and nothing more.

Anyway. The sleepover was really fun. If you would have told me a year ago that I was going to be friends with Mari again, I never would have believed you. But so much has changed now that we do plays together, and it's making me wonder if all those years we weren't friends were maybe just some kind of awkward miscommunication or something. Like maybe she never hated me at all, maybe she was just shy and felt awkward about how to be close again. It felt so natural all hanging out. I really hope that we all keep getting closer. I haven't had good, real, BEST girl friends in SO long. We whispered all night and got all hysterical and psyched out about weird noises, got midnight snacks....We laughed so hard that our ribs hurt, and we could barely breathe. I had forgotten what that was like. By morning we had so many weird inside jokes and sayings and it felt like months and months of friendship development had happened in one night. And, like, all the tension with Mari was suddenly gone. I wish I would have been brave enough to start doing plays sooner so we could have been doing this longer, and I wouldn't have been so lonely. All last year I was just the new, weird, homeschooled art girl and was just kind of without a social group. Everyone else had people they'd gone to middle school with, and elementary school with, and there I was just coming from nowhere, knowing only kids from my neighborhood like Mari, most of whom already had friend groups established.

Last year Mom kept saying how it wasn't true that I didn't know ANYONE at high school because Mari was there, and she'd have Mari's mom tell Mari to hang out with me, but I begged her not to because, hello, that is SO embarrassing. I'd rather just eat alone and walk home by myself after school every day, which is what I did, until now.

Sitting around gossiping on Nora's big squishy couches and hanging out felt so...healthy. That might sound weird, but it did. They're just nice people who like all the same things I like. I felt so comfortable and able to be myself.

Monday, October 2, 11:15 p.m.

Today after dinner I lay in my room in the dark, pretending to smoke a cigarette that was actually just a rolled-up piece of paper and listening to Sigur Rós, and it was relaxing.

Tuesday, October 3, 10:34 p.m.

Today, I stopped in the middle of the trail behind our house as I was walking home from school, and looked around me, like REALLY looked around me for the first time in years. It was so beautiful. All the leaves on the ground were golden and orange and covering everything, and it smelled wet and earthy, and a little bit like woodsmoke. And I felt exhilarated. It felt like an *Our Town* moment.

Last year in Drama 1, Ms. Hanley had us read *Our Town* by Thornton Wilder. And for the whole unit, she drilled into us all of this cliché, moral-of-the-story stuff. And it's cheesy, but I really do feel like that sometimes.

IT'S ABOUT... CHERISHING EVERY MOMENT... LIVING LIFE TO THE FULLEST.

So, an *Our Town* moment is when you look around and feel incredibly alive and notice the beauty around you and feel grateful to be where you are.

I feel like a different person than I was when I started this journal. Like I've matured. I'm so much closer to having the friends I wanted so bad last year, so close to getting to go to parties and have boyfriends and "real" high school experiences.

When I look at my diary entries from last year and even this summer, they feel so babyish and full of banal details about my everyday life. About Roxie and Mom and Dad. And it's not like they're not around or important anymore—but I just feel like there's so many more exciting things happening now with boys and school and plays and friends that I can't bear to waste my time recording those things.

WEDNESDAY, OCTOBER 4, 11 P.M.

The season premiere of *Lost* was today, which meant I had Nora over, because she likes *Lost* too. It was my first time having her over to my house, and I was relieved that Mom and Dad didn't do anything too weird while she was there. I told Dad he should be normal and he said, "Oh, like I should pick my nose in my underwear all night?" and made a goofy face.

Mom made black bean, goat cheese, and sweet potato enchiladas and salad, but we had to all sit around the table to eat before the show started, since Mom considers eating in front of the TV a cardinal sin.

I forgot to say—we got cable! Not the fancy kind, like, we don't have MTV or VH1, but we DO get the main channels and the WB. Roxie said, "Of course once I leave, we finally get cable." Ha! I'm so excited that I can finally watch shows that everyone else at school watches and know what they're talking about, instead of waiting ten billion years for Trek Video or the library to get the DVDs.

When I was younger and Mom was out on errands, I used to put bunny ears on the TV and try to get just enough reception to sneak-watch *Jerry Springer* or *Maury*, but it was always fuzzy.

And now I can sneak-watch them without the fuzz when I get home from school!

Monday, October 9, 10:44 p.m.

I get to design the poster for *Tom Jones*! I jokingly had drawn caricatures of David and Mari (who play the leads) posed like a joke version of those paperback romance novels they sell at the grocery store, because sometimes before drama class starts I draw on the whiteboard and take requests, and Lukas wanted to see Tom and Sophia (David and Mari in the play). I gave David a giant chiseled jaw and boxy chest and cartoonized Mari's boobs bigger and waist smaller than they already are in real life. Everyone thought it was so funny, and when Ms. Hanley came in from the theater she said, "Lord" and rolled her eyes but loved it. Then she said it should be the poster, since the play is a farce. So now I get to make the final version of it and it will be all over TOWN!

Tuesday, October 10, 11:55 p.m.

Today after school Nora and Mari came over, and we hung out and did crafts and then made spaghetti, having a dinner party of sorts since Dad was at some Northwest native plant lecture and Mom is visiting Auntie Eve on her commune in Tallahassee right now. It was fun. I'm starting to get used to having friends again. I'm still amazed that I'm hanging out with Mari, of all people. Every time I hang out with her, it's like more of the distance I've felt between us for the past years and years falls away.

After they left, I painted. I haven't painted (with acrylics) in a long time, and though my picture wasn't exactly as I'd wanted it, I liked the end result. It was a portrait of a boy who I named Ollie (whose head was too big). I don't usually paint at night, but I was "on a roll," as Mom would say. I couldn't get his shirt the way I wanted it, and then I noticed Mom's shredder under her desk was full of all these little paper strips, so I took some out and glued them onto my canvas so it made a cool, collaged, stripy pattern. The way it came together gave me a feeling like I haven't felt in a long time, where the world kind of falls away and my brain quiets, and I work and work without knowing how much time has gone by. My iPod even stopped playing music, but I didn't notice for hours. I took the strips of shredded paper and gave Ollie a halo, arranging them like shining marks around his head.

I only just got in bed, I worked for so long, and I feel so wired, like I could have painted all night.

Thursday, October 12, 10:19 p.m.

I just got back from hanging out with Mari, David, Nora, and Sam, and it was so much fun!

Even though it was a weeknight, we went downtown to this café called Fantasia, which is just about the only other all-ages place we can hang out besides Mallard Ice Cream and Kendrick's.

I had seen that they were having a poetry night, so we decided to check it out. It was packed and there were tons of cool, hip college students and people sitting around little tables and all over the floor.

We all got "London Fogs" because they sounded sophisticated and cozy. I immediately burnt my tongue off on the steamed milk, but it was sooo good. It was so fun to be at a café at night—it made me feel very European and cool. I wondered if everyone older there thought we were their age. The poets who performed were incredible. I'd never really heard poetry like that, or much at all really. I always thought that poems needed to be rhyme-y and stuff, but these were just people talking about their lives and it was so beautiful I wanted to cry, like really emotional, magical monologues, and instead of clapping when people were done, everyone snapped.

Afterward we walked around downtown to stay warm, putting off calling our parents for rides because we were all having such a nice time. We were all so bowled over by how incredible it was, so we vowed to try to go every week if we could. Sam and I fell into step beside each other, and he said, "I bet you'd be good at doing poetry." I laughed and asked why he would think that because he has absolutely no evidence to prove it, but he just shrugged.

I was so surprised to hear that Sam Goldman had any thoughts about me at all, let alone really nice ones. It made my stomach go flip-flop and my cheeks go red.

I realized that as we'd been talking, we had accidentally sped up way ahead of the group and were almost a block ahead, alone. I told him that I bet he'd be good too. He does look a bit like a young Allen Ginsberg after all.

Sunday, October 15, 10:10 p.m.

I spent the weekend at Roxie's, which was so fun! I took the Greyhound to Seattle, where she met me at the downtown station, then we ate Top Ramen and her friends Miles and Jason came over to

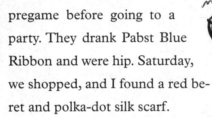

pregame before going to a party. They drank Pabst Blue Ribbon and were hip. Saturday, we shopped, and I found a red beret and polka-dot silk scarf.

Then, that night we saw Sufjan Stevens at the Paramount Theatre. It was soooo amazing.

The Paramount is like a festival of gilded balconies and glowing, glittery chandeliers. There were swarms of extremely cool people in attendance, and before the show we picked out our favorite outfits. I might try to replicate some of them with things I find at Value Village when I get home.

SOME OF OUR FAVE OUTFITS

The show itself was incredible of course. Words can't even describe it.

After the show it was SO cold out, and I only had my velvet jacket that doesn't button all the way up and ballet flats that are basically just slivered almonds. We ran home to the warmth of Roxie's, then ate pink and white animal cookies, cuddled under a blanket on her gold 70s couch. Roxie always has good snacks around that Mom would never allow.

SUNDAY, OCTOBER 22, 12:23 A.M.

Sorry I haven't written all week. It's amazingly autumn-y here. Everything is really quiet and muffled from the fog outside. It feels like the rain and storms are right around the corner and I can't wait.

I just got home from the homecoming dance, where I was taking yearbook pictures with Asher. He picked me up in one of his Subarus so that Dad didn't have to drive me. I could tell Mom wanted to ask if he was my date but was biting it back, thank GOD. She spared me from having to tell her for the gazillionth time that no, I do not in fact have a date, that tonight is, in fact, "work."

The first thing Asher said to me when I got in was, "Dum Dum?" To which I said, "Excuse me?"

But instead of responding he threw a little Dum Dum lollypop at me (pineapple) and then popped one into his own mouth.

I told him about the Sufjan Stevens show last weekend, because he hadn't been in class last week, and he said "Cool" in his signature smirky, unsurprised way, as if he already knew all about it, which I know he didn't because I'd been saving it up so I could reveal I'd gone as if it was no big deal.

Then he said, "I thought 'Casimir Pulaski Day' sounded almost as good live as it does on the album, did you?" and I said, "What do you mean you thought?" but he just winked. "Were you there???" He shrugged. "I saw you at intermission with your sister. She seems cool."

I was flabbergasted. Why hadn't he said hi to me?? I mean…I know why, because he's ultra cool and probably didn't want to associate with me because he was with friends who are older and hip. Also figures that he would like Roxie, everyone does. Then he asked what my favorite song off Sufjan's new album is. (It's "Pittsfield.") And I asked him where he was last week, and he just said, "Recording." "Like with your band?" I asked, and he said, "Yupperino." Apparently they were in Seattle all week working with a real recording studio. I can't believe he just skips school to go play with his band. Don't his parents care? Although from what Annie said about his parents, I wouldn't be surprised if they don't. It sounds like they're mega chill to a wild extent.

I kept wondering if all the things Annie said about him were true. He can be pretty suave. But also, just so strange.

Not much can be said about the dance. All the lights were turned off in the school cafeteria, and the cheerleaders had hung limp crepe paper around and painted a sign to make it seem less like everyone was just dancing in…the cafeteria with the lights turned off. It was sweaty and dark and loud, and the air was practically electric with teenage sexual tension. Asher and I were the only people in Yearbook who weren't going with dates, which is why we got stuck with the job of taking pictures. I dressed up a little bit, but not in, like, formal wear. Asher was just wearing his usual kind of funky, grungy clothes, including a T-shirt that had the words MEDIOCRE SEX written off-center in Sharpie on it. He's so weird. The cheerleaders taking tickets gave him VERY skeptical,

disgusted looks when we showed them our "press passes" (notes from our teacher) but let us in anyway. If it was up to them, boys probably wouldn't be able to even set foot in the school without a popped-collar polo shirt on, let alone come to a dance without a suit.

I wonder if people thought we were there as a couple. The idea made me a little embarrassed, considering his outfit, but also I didn't TOTALLY mind the thought, mostly because I think most people think I'm like a celibate widow hermit so the idea of proving them wrong was a little bit of a thrill.

I don't know why Asher wasn't there with Sarah Sokolowski, who I'm pretty sure he's dating. She's probably too cool for things like dances.

I saw almost everyone from drama at the dance: David, who couldn't find his date; Jenna, who was happy without one; Mari and her date, Jordan; and Lukas, who came up to me dejectedly, trying to avoid his cheerleader date, who, apparently, he hates. (Why didn't he and Mari go together??) Sam was there with a girl named Kayla, who goes to a different school. No Owen. I wonder if he was deep in the throng of grinding dancers? Probably with Annie or one of her other friends. Having the big fancy Yearbook camera gave me a purpose and made me not feel as awkward as I would have if I had just been there on my own.

Asher and I mostly were off on our own getting photos, but we occasionally met up to hang out on the outskirts and make fun of drunk jocks trying to bump and grind. A few times Asher pretended to dance to the music, ironically going out on to the dance floor and making goofy faces at me while grinding up behind the jocks (without actually touching

them)! A couple times he tried to jokingly pull me in to dance with him, but I
pretended to be all "Nooo,
I can't" because I HATE
dancing and am incredi-
bly bad at it. Plus, we had
our cameras, and he
has a girlfriend! And
I don't like him that
way anyway.

I finally caught a glimpse of Owen, deep in the tangle of sweaty, squirm-
ing bodies. I couldn't tell who he was with, though. I kept imagining him
emerging from the throng, sweat misting his brow and his tie loosened,
saying, "Oh, are you here without a date? Me too!" and then pulling me
in to dance....

Maybe he had wanted to ask me that day that we walked home together,
but I'd ruined it?

Anyway, I'm falling asleep now. I'll write more later. I haven't even
told you about Friday yet!

11:34 A.m.

Okay, so Friday night (the day before homecoming) Nora, Mari, David,
and I got all dressed up in dresses and suits like glamorous beatniks and
went downtown to see *The Science of Sleep* at the Pickford cinema.

We kept speaking with French accents all night, pretending we were exchange students from Paris. Once Nora warms up and starts to be less shy, she is SO good at accents—she even had the hot hipster college student who works at the movie theater convinced.

152

The movie was simply incroyable and so surreal. It was one of those movies that I wanted to live inside. It made me ache, it was so beautiful and perfect. I think everyone else liked it but mostly thought it was weird. It felt like I had seen something in a language that only I spoke, and they'd been able to mostly follow along but hadn't quite GOTTEN it like I had. Maybe I will ask for the soundtrack CD for Xmas. Nora and David had never even been to the Pickford before! Finally Mom dragging me to, like, every 17-hour documentary and slow-ass subtitled Danish drama for homeschool is coming in handy and making me seem cool and alternative for bringing them there.

After the movie, we bused to Mari's and talked for hours around a bunch of her mom's candles, asking random questions and having deep, philosophical conversations. David and Nora left around 10, and then Sam came over, and we sat on the couch under a blanket all cozy.

I've been hanging out with Sam a bit more since the play started. He was in *Thoreau* (he played my son, Thoreau's brother), but we barely ever talked. I thought of him as just being one of the drama-elite boys, and he never struck my fancy like David and Owen and even Lukas did then. But lately during rehearsals I've started to notice him a little more, I think because we play siblings in *Tom Jones* and have a lot of entrances together, so we interact more. I think I'm starting to like him a little bit. As much as I hate it, I am. I hate it because Nora likes him too....And I don't want to be THAT friend, who steals crushes. She confessed it to me the other day when we were walking to my house after rehearsal.

I didn't have the heart to tell her I've started liking him too...and that I'm kind of over Owen for the most part. Everyone likes Sam. He's one of the most likable people in the universe. I can't help it. The more I get to know him and become better friends with him, the more I'm attracted to him. He's so comfortable and makes really steady eye contact. Not like David's intense, squinty eye contact that feels like he's trying to scan the deepest parts of your inner soul, just assuring and kind of LISTENING. If you can listen with your eyes.

That night I told him and Mari about my *Our Town* moments. About the other day when I was walking down the trail and felt so alive and present and moment cherish-y. And they said they knew exactly what I meant...!

ON SUNDAY, I WAS DOING HOMEWORK IN MY ROOM, AND MY CAT WAS ON THE BED IN A PERFECT LITTLE RAY OF SUNLIGHT. SHE'S ALL BLACK BUT WHEN THE SUN SHINES ON HER, YOU CAN SEE ALL THIS GOLDEN AND BROWN IN HER FUR. I TOOK A BREAK AND JUST LAID WITH HER FOR A MINUTE, AND IT TOTALLY FELT LIKE THAT, LIKE THE MOST IMPORTANT THING TO DO WAS BE STILL AND SOAK UP THE BEAUTY OF THE EXACT MOMENT I WAS IN.

Mari nodded, and we all went quiet. Sam and I were making eye contact. And I felt this thing in my chest, like I wanted to cry. Like a deep pang of love and gratefulness that they understood. I don't really tell anyone about *Our Town* moments, not even Roxie because I think most people won't get it. Or think I'm just being overly melodramatic and romantic. But Sam and Mari got it. And that made me happy.

We were so immersed in our candle gazing and talking that I didn't notice what time it was, and when I looked at my phone it was 4 A.M.!!!!!!!!!!!! And I had FIVE missed calls from Mom.

I felt a sinking in the pit of my stomach that almost ruined the whole night because I've never been so late for my curfew before, and so I didn't know what Mom was going to do. We all quickly hugged goodbye, and I ran as fast as I could home. I'm always creeped out walking home from Mari's late at night. You either have to walk down the trail or past a giant haunted Victorian mansion on the street, but tonight I flew down the trail without time to be scared.

Mom was waiting up for me and was mostly just annoyed that I hadn't been paying attention to my phone and telling her what was going on, and that she was still up at "this hour."

But that's about it, and we just went to bed and I could tell she was VERY mad but wasn't going to do anything about it, and sure enough in the morning everything was fine. Phew!!!! I'm so glad I don't have parents who are SO strict. Mom just makes me feel guilty when I breach her trust and don't tell her my plan or waste her time, like I did last night. But I'd take guilt any day over being grounded.

MONDAY, OCTOBER 23, 10:08 P.M.

I must stop liking Sam. And yet I really don't want to. Everything about him feels like a dream. He's such an amazing actor and is just so...irresistible. But it's not just me—I think he's the new Lukas. As in, EVERYONE in drama falls in love with him at some point. Just the other day Annie kept asking me if I thought Sam was looking at her. And I couldn't tell if he was, or if he was looking at me, because we were sitting next to each other the whole class. And I know that Nora at least used to like him, and maybe still does. The funny thing is, when I think about it, I think he's actually the first guy I've liked who I didn't like JUST because I had some tiny vain thought that he liked me first. Not that I think he dislikes me, he has definitely shown interest, but it feels like it's been in a more friendship-y way. Like I've actually taken time to get to know him before falling immediately in love. But now that I'm noticing him, he's kind of like...a sex god. He's like this perfect Greek statue that I want to touch...not in a dirty way, but in, like...an artistic way....Everything about him just gets to me.

It seems like, judging by my family, politics, and hobbies, he would be my "type." And maybe he is, but I'm probably not his....He probably likes loud, outgoing, experienced girls like Annie. Or gorgeous, goofball stoner-y girls like Jenna...or maybe he's into Mari...which...get in line.

♡ ♡ SAM GOLDMAN ♡ ♡

SLIGHT FURROWED BROW AT ALL TIMES LIKE HE'S PONDERING SOME COMPLEX EQUATION

BEAUTIFUL DARK HAIR

CHISELED JAW

CUTE SCHOLARLY GLASSES

WOOLLY SWEATER

THERMOS OF COFFEE BECAUSE HE'S ALWAYS UP ALL NIGHT DOING HOMEWORK

GIANT HEAVY BACKPACK BECAUSE HE TAKES 2367895 SUPER-ADVANCED CLASSES AND IS EXTREMELY SCHOLASTIC

DORKY SHOES THAT ARE ALWAYS FALLING APART BECAUSE HE ONLY WEARS ONE PAIR AND THEY GET WORN TO DEATH

TATTERED CORDUROYS

Sam is Jewish but his family is more observant than mine and Mari's. "You could say you're semi-Semites," he said the other day when I told him that Mari and I celebrate Christmas, in addition to Hanukkah, every year. "Or...Jew-ISH," I said, and he momentarily unfurrowed his brow to smile (!!!). He is so serious that all I want to do is try to make him laugh.

His mom is a literature professor at the university, his dad is some kind of fancy specialist doctor, and he has a sister who's much younger, like seven years old (cute!!). He hasn't dated anyone in the drama group that I know of, though I know he's really good friends with Jenna so it's possible they've hooked up....I don't think he's TOO much of a hardcore partier because he's intensely into doing well in school, and I think he is on some rigorous academic track to become a doctor or professor or something. He's in a bunch of AP classes and always seems to have more homework than everyone else. And when he's not doing homework he's always reading plays and books, and even works a few hours a week at the Toy Jungle, where he gets to test out new board games and stuff. In plays he's usually the "straight man," which he says is why he likes his role in *Tom Jones*, because he gets to play a goofy character for a change. When he isn't serious, his sense of humor is kind of sarcastic and intellectual—"Dry, British humor," he says, like *Mr. Bean* and *Fawlty Towers*, which are his favorites (besides Star Wars). He even wants to perform a Mr. Bean skit at the State Thespian competition someday.

I keep doing this thing where I try to distract myself from liking Sam by telling myself I like Owen still. I think to try to avoid disappointment with Sam...and because I feel a little bad just dropping Owen now that Sam's my new crush. Like I built him up for so long, I pined about him to so many people and was so obsessed and in love with him, that I almost feel a little silly just moving on to someone else...like, was I just delusional? Did I ever really like him? Was any of it real? Now that things feel so intense with Sam, liking Owen feels like it was ages ago. Part of me thinks I need to keep liking him forever and just dig in my heels so I don't come off as some will-o'-the-wisp girl who just flits from crush to crush like a slutty honeybee in a field of flowers.

It doesn't help that Sam doesn't have a Myspace. It gives me one less way to obsess and be a creep over him and so ALL of that stalker energy ends up going to Owen because his profile is just THERE and so familiar. I keep going through his photos to see if there's any with Sam. But he doesn't do much on Myspace, so there's nothing to stalk. Just the same three tiny fuzzy photos of him doing ballet and acting in a play last summer and sailing that have been there, unchanged, for like 26930498 years.

I see both of them at fall play rehearsals every day. But I mostly only have eyes for Sam now. Before I started liking him I thought being in the play together would rekindle things with Owen. But liking Owen started to feel like a chore, like trying in vain to get closer to someone who will always be far away. Every interaction we'd have would end in awkwardness or mystery, just like the infamous car ride last summer. Yesterday I was looking back at my old entries from last summer and thinking how I'm starting to feel totally over him. Been there, done that, old flame… But then as I read and remembered *Thoreau* and the tension backstage… and what WAS the deal with that car ride where he asked for my number? Where he was so flirty then nothing happened? It's funny too that Sam is a part of that story, a part of it that I never paid any attention to before, since he is the one Owen called in the car. I wonder if he has another side of the story, more intel on how Owen felt about me then. Not that I would ever ask him, because it might make him think I'm still into Owen and not him. Although that could be good to make him jealous…?

It is just SO hard to completely let go of that teeny, dull glow of hope that Owen likes me. Or liked me. And sometimes even David too. The hope keeps ALMOST being burnt out. But even WITH my crush on Sam, sometimes it ignites again just the teeniest bit.

I think I just want SO badly for it to be true. To prove something. To myself maybe. That I'm likable. Lovable. DESIRABLE.

I just want to be the girl in the movie for once. Even though I know I'll never be a hip ingenue like Charlotte Gainsbourg in *The Science of Sleep*. I think it's why I like to put music on sometimes and pretend like I'm in a movie, that my gaze is the camera panning around my room or outside, and then imagining it settling on me. On my lips, or eyes, or hair, like behind the camera there's someone thinking I'm the most beautiful and interesting creature they've ever seen.

I sound so annoying and narcissistic. I need sleep!!!
Only 12 hours till I see Sam…

TUESDAY, OCTOBER 24, 9:13 P.M.

We finally got the set finished for the play! Hanley said I should be on the set-building crew because I'm "so good at art." I thought I'd get to be creative—but it turned out to just be Nora and me sponge-painting big cartoony trees cut out of plywood green and brown. Not exactly ART but it was still fun because we were all at the theater after hours at night, which felt exciting and bad even though it was allowed and Ms. Hanley was there.

Sam was there too, lifting sheets of plywood and screwing things together with Lukas and Mr. Cobb, the math teacher, who helps build everything for the plays. Sam also does all the light setting with the techs and seems to know where everything is in the theater. The teachers talk to him like he's one of them, rather than a student. Probably because he seems so responsible.

I'm so excited for our final dress and tech rehearsals this week, now that we have the set. It looks sooo pro, especially with the lighting too.

It's going to be my first "real" show on the "real" stage, since the summer play was at the Firehouse Performing Arts Center, which is more just a big room that's mostly used for dance shows and events. I'm starting to get nervous!!!

Thursday, October 26, 10:31 p.m.

Updates, updates, updates.

I'm slowly (well, not slowly) but surely falling in love with Sam. The more we hang out, the more everything with Owen kind of fades into the background.

I have kind of an established friend group of drama people now. It's Mari, Nora, Annie, Sam, and David. Lukas and Jenna and the others kind of rotate in and out of hangouts, but the core group usually stays the same. We stay late at the Little Theater after rehearsals or walk to my or Mari's house, where we've been piling on couches to joke and philosophize and lie around. We talk about nature and literature, theater, art, everything imaginable, and people. We talk a lot about people, but not in a behind-the-back, mean way (most of the time), just in an analytical way....Sam and Nora always get very disapproving when the conversation gets into gossip territory, which Annie or I am usually responsible for, being rowdier than Mari, who's so sweet and more of an introvert. I'm coming to realize that I think most of the times I thought she was too cool for me, she was just being shy, and maybe *I* was the one who was shunning HER last year and at the beginning of *Thoreau*....

Anyway. Even though it's a school night, Nora, Mari, Sam, and I all hung out tonight after the free student preview performance of *Tom Jones*, which was spectacular. I could see Asher taking photos for Yearbook out of the corner of my eye while I was onstage. I wonder if he liked the show, or if he thinks it was so dorky.

my COSTUME, I GET To WEAR A WIG!

Mom and Dad were out at dinner and a movie with Mari's parents tonight, so we were all alone at my house. We cooked dinner then ended up cuddled in my bed just talking and eating the candy Mom bought for Halloween (no trick-or-treaters ever come to our house because it's too hard to find, so I doubt we'll need it). I love being so comfortable around people. We hug a lot, which I've never done with friends before, and it's like family. I think this must be what grown-up friendships are like, although I never see my parents lying in bed laughing for hours with their friends. I wonder if they ever did.

Things are starting to feel so tense backstage with Sam. A lot like things were with Owen during *Thoreau*, but deeper and more intense. There's some weird magic that kicks in when a play goes from just being a rehearsal to being a show. Having an audience changes everything. My heart was skipping around so wild as we heard everyone coming into the theater, and I thought I was gonna black out and forget all my lines. I always feel like I have to pee right before I go onstage. Sam was standing next to me because we go on together in one of the first scenes. It was like I could feel vibrations radiating off of him and zapping me. When we're standing in the wings, whispering before we go on, it's like everything else, and everyone else in the show, disappears. That's how it feels when we make eye contact too, like I'm sinking and sinking and I can't get out, like a fire alarm could go off and I'd never even notice. I just keep wondering if he feels it too.

I asked Mari as we walked to my house after school the other day if she thought tension like that COULD exist between people if it wasn't mutual. Like, is it something that CAN be one-sided? Or does it require that both people feel it for it to exist at all? She said she thought it had to be mutual, that it feels different when you like someone and they don't like you back. She said it feels that way with her and Lukas sometimes, like there's some intense force pulling them together and resistance is futile, but that when they actually try to make things happen, it's like when you put the wrong sides of two magnets together and instead of

snapping into place they hover in a tense dance, unable to get close. So, if she thinks it has to be mutual for the feeling to exist, that means Sam MUST like me too. And that means Owen must have liked me, for that matter. And maybe David as well…Or maybe those DID feel different, like she said it does when someone doesn't like you back. But it's hard to remember. It's all so confusing, and so clouded by what I want. Or wanted at the time. I wish it wasn't so awkward just to ask someone how they feel.

SUNDAY, OCTOBER 29, 12:34 P.M.

Last night Annie had a Halloween party. It was my first time going to her house. I guess I assumed she was really rich or something, I think because I know Jenna is and they're such good friends. But it was just a normal, funky old house, not even too far away from mine. Her parents bought us pizza and then went out to a party of their own. Nothing too eventful happened during the party. I had wondered if it was going to be really wild, because I know Annie has partied with Lukas and Owen and Sam at Jenna's parties at her lake house. But there weren't even beers or anything.

RED LIPSTICK

SKIMPY VINTAGE PINK SLIP

FAKE CIGARETTE THAT I "BORROWED" FROM THE DRAMA ROOM PROP CLOSET (IT PUFFS FAKE SMOKE WHEN YOU BLOW ON IT), WHICH MAKES ME FEEL TRÈS SOPHISTIQUÉ.

ELBOW-LENGTH STRETCHY VELVET GLOVES

PILLOW THAT I SPONTANEOUSLY STUFFED UP MY DRESS TO MAKE A PREGNANCY BUMP

MY "CHARACTER SHOES" FOR PLAYS

FISHNET STOCKINGS

When I arrived at the party, David asked what I was, and I randomly blurted out, "The Virgin Mary" and took a moody draw off my fake cigarette, and everyone laughed. It was really fun, even though Sam wasn't there 😣. Or Owen.

I heard Jenna say that they were at some other party across town, and that they were maybe going to drop by.

Leave it to Nora to be so pure and sweet on a night when all the rest of us are dressing slutty! Nathan came, with Tim (to Jenna's excitement), dressed up as the guys from *Pulp Fiction*, and Freya, who does tech for our plays. Lukas only came by briefly but no Sam. Sigh. My heart almost jumped out of my body when I saw Lukas walk in, since I thought they might be together. He was "a soccer player" with some jersey on and shorts. Hot guys get away with the most ridiculous stuff. It was just his regular clothes but maybe a teeny bit sportier. Jenna and Annie kept clinging on to him, trying to get him to stay. Annie complained all night about how she wished more people would come and how much funner it would be if there were more boys and someone had brought booze. Even when it was her own party, she was acting too cool. Every time we'd be rowdy and having fun playing drama games or goofing around, she'd roll her eyes and loudly say, "You guys are so weird, I need a smoke," all exhausted like we were high-energy toddlers wearing down her sensitive nerves, then she'd dramatically go outside to the front porch as if she wanted one of us to be scandalized and tell her not to. Jenna and David went out to smoke a few times with her. I wonder if they do it all the time. But they didn't have their own cigarettes like Annie did. I can't believe they smoked cigarettes right on the porch when Annie's parents could have come home at ANY TIME, or

someone who knows her could have walked by. Mom would have me packed off to rehab in Switzerland if she even knew I was PRETEND-ING to smoke tonight.

I think Annie felt insecure that all of us would THINK she was the kind of person to throw such a tame and un-scandalous party, even though WE were all that type of person to be there and were having a great time.

We all played Mafia and Catch Phrase then watched *Rocky Horror Picture Show* and ate popcorn and candy corn and peanut butter cups.

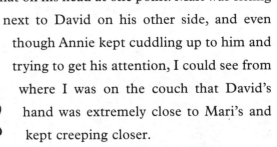

Annie kept grabbing David during the movie and react-ing dramatically to everything, screaming or laughing extra loud. She kept whispering things to him and Jenna during the movie too, and even put her pleather cab driver hat on his head at one point. Mari was sitting next to David on his other side, and even though Annie kept cuddling up to him and trying to get his attention, I could see from where I was on the couch that David's hand was extremely close to Mari's and kept creeping closer.

I didn't even know they liked each other. He continued to play along with An-nie's hijinks, though—he's such a player. I can't believe I ever liked him. I just kept wondering what Sam was up to and what kind of party he was at. I was distracted throughout the whole movie wishing he was there so we could be cuddled under a blanket too. I'm just so afraid

that if things don't progress before the play is over, nothing will come of our romance (if that's what you can even call it) and he'll lose interest. I'm afraid it will be Owen all over again, and that without the tension of backstage whispers it will all just slip away and fade. Him not being here tonight feels like time wasted. The play will end, and he'll realize I'm just a dork nobody, a loser homeschooled artist girl who knows every obscure Harry Potter character's name by heart. I wonder what he dressed up as tonight, and if he's wondering what I dressed up as....I wonder what girls are at the party he's at, and if he likes any of them.

Me, Mari, Jenna, David, and Nora ended up sleeping over at Annie's house. I could tell Jenna was sad that Nathan didn't stay too. Nora and Jenna were on Annie's bed and me, Annie, Mari, and David were on the floor. I conveniently "forgot" to tell Mom that David was sleeping over too....

We were all awake till like 5 a.m. talking and laughing. Then, the wildest thing happened. After most people had finally conked out, at about 6 or 7 a.m. I woke up to the harmonious sounds of smacking lips.

At first, I wasn't even sure what the sound was. I thought maybe Annie's dog had gotten in and was licking something near me, but my heart started racing for some reason and I felt my face go red, like my body knew before I did what was going on. I felt frozen, like I shouldn't look, but I wanted to know SO bad who it was, and finally I turned over for half a second and saw MARI AND DAVID making out on their sleeping bags next to me.

I think I was the only one who saw. I'm pretty sure everyone else was asleep. Annie had her back turned and seemed to be asleep. In the morning, I ended up telling her what I'd seen....

To which Sam later said, "You may as well have broadcast the news on BBC, Fox, and Al Jazeera." I know I shouldn't have...but I think I felt kind of bad for her and wanted her to know. Because it was so clear that she liked him, and even though Annie can be annoying, it felt cruel to leave her in the dark about what had happened right next to her while she was sleeping, and in her own house, with the boy that everyone knows she likes.

When I told her, it seemed like a flash of hurt briefly crossed her face, and then she raised her eyebrows and grinned and yelled, "OHHHH MY GOD, MARI AND DAVID WERE GETTING FRISKY?????" in a kind of over-the-top, gleeful, rowdy way. I couldn't tell if she was really upset or not, and she kept bringing it up to everyone for the rest of the day. I think Mari was embarrassed that I told Annie, and a little mad. And I felt kind of icky about it. Like I'd betrayed her. But I felt a little upset by the make-out too. And maybe I was getting some kind of revenge for that, even though I hadn't really intended to. I'm not upset because I still like David or anything—that ship has long sailed. More because of the sheer nerve of them making out RIGHT NEXT TO ME, and in someone else's house!! I felt like it was a breach of our friendship or something. I can't really explain it. It's just how I felt. I still feel bad that I told Annie, though, even though part of me wonders if she hadn't been sleeping either and already knew. She just didn't seem that surprised when I told her.

I think maybe I was a little jealous too. Mari didn't even like David and she knew Annie did. It seems like she just made out with him because he was just…there. And all I kept thinking was that I wished it was me. Not with David, but with Sam. I just wish he'd been there so we could have been the ones hooking up, the ones everyone was talking about the next day. Not that I want to be gossiped about, but I want to be the one doing wild and exciting things for once. It felt so weird to watch my friend do something that I didn't even know she wanted to do. I didn't even know she had feelings for him and yet there she was, as if it was nothing. As if making out with someone is just easy as pie, when for me, it's something I've never done in my whole life. That I want SO badly to experience with a boy I like. With Sam.

SamSamSamSamSamSam. Why wasn't he there??

SATURDAY, NOVEMBER 4, 11:40 A.M.

Last night was our OFFICIAL opening night of *Tom Jones*! The show went really well. It was a completely full house, and all the audience members were really responsive. The tension with Sam backstage felt, if possible, even more intense than usual because of the crowd's energy, like it could be cut with a knife.

When we do the warm-up rituals, we always stand next to each other in the circle. After the huddle, everyone goes around and whispers, "Break a leg" to each member of the cast while they link pinkies and mock kiss each other on the cheek twice, like in France. You have to keep eye contact with the person when you say it or it's bad luck. And for some reason, Sam and I keep saving each other for last. And the eye contact we make feels extra heavy. Like he's trying to tell me something. And I'm probably imaging it, but I could swear that his lips almost grazed my cheeks when we did the air kisses, and no one else's ever do.

He smells so good I could die. Like coffee and peppermint deodorant and sweat, and the baby powder he puts in his hair before the show to make it look gray.

Backstage I told him about the Halloween party, and he said, "I'm sad I couldn't make it." I couldn't tell if he was just saying that to be nice, or if it was because he wishes we could have hooked up. I asked where he was and he said he was carving pumpkins with his little sister (CUTE), and then later he and Owen went to a party with a bunch of people from cross-country, which they both do. I think it's the same party Lukas went to after ours too. He asked what I was, and when I told him he said, "That's a little crass, don't you think?" but was smiling, so I knew he was teasing. Then, "I wish I could have seen it, though." I could have died.

I asked what he was and he said he was "long-shot 2004 presidential candidate Howard Dean" and that he just wore a button-up shirt and tie and went around screaming, "Yeaah!" in a high-pitched voice. I have no idea what he was talking about but laughed and pretended I did because I think it was supposed to be a joke.

NOTE TO SELF: GET SMARTER ABOUT POLITICAL-Y THINGS SO SAM THINKS I'm COOL!

Mom and Dad came to the show, and even Roxie came all the way from Seattle with her hip friend Miles. After it was over, when everyone was pouring out of the theater, Asher Wilson came up to me and said, "Good job!" and I said, "Thanks." I was surprised he was there because he already saw the show when he photographed the school matinee for Yearbook, so it was his second time. He looked like he wanted to say something more and gave me kind of an awkward side-hug. But then Annie and Jenna pulled me away to be in a group photo with Ms. Hanley and the whole cast and crew and I lost track of him.

But, in other news.

I'm falling in love.

Or maybe I'm IN love, and it's for the first time. Because I see now that the others don't matter, and although I say that every time, I know that this time it's true.

After the show David, Mari, Nora, Annie, and Sam all came over to my house, because Roxie is home and she made us all dinner. Then after we ate we all went up and lay in my bed, which was nice if slightly uncomfortable since it was six people on a twin. Nora was lying between Sam and me and my arm was kind of draped over her and resting on Sam's chest. All the lights were off except my lava lamp, and we listened to Sigur Rós, who none of them had even heard of before, and talked and talked about how the show had gone.

After a while I got self-conscious that my hand was on Sam's chest and over Nora's body, so I drew it back. I whispered, "Sorry," then Sam whispered, "It's okay," and he took my hand and put it back on his chest (!).

Sometimes I'd feel his arm or cheek and they were perfectly soft, and sometimes he'd touch my hand, running a thumb lightly over it, which made me feel electric inside. Then at one point, he took my hand and

WE HELD HANDS.

Intertwining our fingers and just feeling every inch of the other person's hand. Sometimes I'd press harder and he'd press harder and our fingers would explore each other's like skinny starfish.

If he ever had to reach up and take his hand away,

he'd always come back. Sometimes we would make eye contact, but mostly we were quiet and looking at the others, talking and joking like nothing was happening. And I wonder if they noticed, noticed that we had disappeared into this bubble, where my skin tingled and nothing was important except Sam and his perfect hands and perfect skin and perfect brown eyes.

Finally, the music turned off and the lights went on, and we went downstairs and neither of us said anything out loud. And when he hugged me good night, it was so hard it was both like my bones were being crushed and like I was melting into him, and I wanted him to kiss me. So bad. And it's exactly six hours until I see him again.

Monday, November 6, 2:56 p.m.

Our last show was Sunday. It went really well, and we had a very full house, especially for a Sunday matinee. Last time I wrote was a bit ago. Sam's and my relationship has...progressed, I suppose.

Backstage we stand together and lean on each other, and once he even put his arm around me. On Saturday, I was getting out of costume, and David came up to me.

SO ARE YOU AND SAM AN ITEM??

So began David taunting me about Sam and me. It really rattled me, to think that people could actually think we are together and were talking about us. Sometimes I forget that I'm a person in the world who other people see and think about. Sometimes I forget that Sam, and everything going on between us, isn't just some fantasy I've cooked up. And that the moments we have together backstage, or while we're getting into costume, or after the show that feel so intimate, and quiet, are seen or overheard by other people. Are gossiped about.

Anyway. Saturday was "Guys' Night," which is a Little Theater tradition of going to Mallard Ice Cream then Kendrick's to play pool after the show. Mari told me it's called Guys' Night because it used to be "boys only," but then she and a bunch of other girls her freshman year started a tradition of crashing their hangouts, so now it's for everyone in the show but the name stuck.

At Kendrick's, Mari approached me about Sam and me. Saying she'd heard that we'd been "seen" holding hands and that we were "always together."

I haven't talked to her much since Halloween. I think because I still feel a little weird about what happened at Annie's house. And I feel guilty for telling Annie. And I feel like she's just kind of been off with David ever since. Even though I had no idea she even liked him, they seem to be together now...or at least hanging out a lot. I've noticed Lukas giving them a lot of sad puppy dog looks while we're all getting into costume for the play.

But I was just bursting at the seams to tell someone about what's been going on with Sam, so I spilled my heart to her, and it was just like a dam had broken, and suddenly things between us were normal again. I even told her about the hand-holding incident. And Mari got really excited.

I asked her what's going on with David, and she said that everything with him just happened so fast. That she had been so focused on Lukas being her longtime crush that she'd never really noticed David before, but once he was expressing interest she went along with it because why not, and that it felt nice. Apparently he's been taking her on fancy dates and they're kind of a "thing." She said she felt bad about the way things went on Halloween, though, and that Annie is pissed at her and being passive aggressive, pretending not to care. "And she's just sucking up to David, not being mad at him at all, even though he was the one who initiated the whole thing," she said. I told her I was sorry I told Annie. And she said it was okay. That Annie would have found out somehow anyway.

It was so nice to talk to her. Not talking even for a week made me realize what good friends we've become again. I've been hanging out with Nora, but talking to her about boys just isn't the same. I know she still likes Sam a little bit, and so I've been afraid of telling her what's going on. Even though she probably knows already since she was between us when we held hands on my bed. Which I also feel kind of weird and guilty about. Because it felt so intimate, I kind of forgot she was there after a while, and I feel bad about that. But it's not like we had sex in front of her or something, we only held hands!!

Last week I asked her how "far" she thought everyone in the play had gone. I wanted to go through and speculate just for fun. But she just said, "I don't really think about that sort of thing." And changed the subject. Like some kind of goddamn puritan robot! How can you not wonder?? Like am I some pervert Harriet the Spy?? Since I basically want to know everything about everyone at all times? I feel like she's in denial that, like it or not, we're almost grown-ups now. And that means sex. It's NORMAL to be hooking up and being wild, and she acts like people who even thinks about it are heathen peasants rolling in the fields.

After the last show on Sunday (Mom and Dad came again, this time with flowers for me! And Grandma too), we all gathered in the Little Theater with Ms. Hanley for a last circle-up before striking the set. I can't believe it's over already; it feels like it went so fast. And yet, I'm a completely different person than I was when the show began. To think at auditions I was still mooning over Owen, and now I barely pay him any mind. It was only a few months ago, and I had no idea that by this time I'd have held hands with a boy, and maybe (hopefully) be on my way to more....

After strike and cleaning up the drama room, where all our makeup and costumes and props are stored, parents came to pick us up and we went to Nora's for the CAST PARTY.

Nora offered to host because she has a big living room that can fit lots of people and a giant yard that backs up to the woods that's good for playing outdoor games. She even has a swing that's attached to two giant trees like 70 feet up. There's a rope attached to the seat of the swing that two or three people have to pull while you're sitting on it, so it lifts you waaaayyyy up into the air, and when they let you go it's the scariest thing, you think you're going to pee your pants. You whiz backward into the forest over a giant ravine. I was too scared to do it at first, but everyone in the cast was having a go, so finally I tried it, and it was one of the most exhilarating things I've ever done.

Annie would make a really big deal of it every time she went on, screaming and screaming then clinging on to Lukas and David and any boy nearby when she got off like she was going to faint. Then Lukas and Sam started doing the swing standing up, and with no hands and stuff, and Nora got really mad and called the whole thing off, because she's such a safety stickler. I was relieved, though, because it was kind of scary.

Apparently, the cast parties used to be at Jenna's house, like the one Nora told me about, but the last one got too wild and a bunch of kids got in trouble for drinking, and Ms. Hanley had to ban them from happening there because the whole cast goes, even puny freshmen, and they're kind of "affiliated" with the show, and she didn't want the school to be liable for any "funny business." I think Ms. Hanley knew that there would definitely be "no funny business" (i.e., drinking) at Nora's.

Nothing really big happened with Sam and me at the cast party…except I wanted him more than ever before. Like my body was on fire, and he was the only thing that could quench the flame. I wore my new white vintage sweater and my perfect red 80s flats I got at Value Village and felt very cute.

Toward the end of the night, I sat next to him on the couch and he put his arm around me, and we were kind of leaning on each other, like a couple, I suppose, kind of spooning sitting up. Then WE HELD HANDS AGAIN. People were staring but I didn't care because I felt so warm and safe and happy and electric inside. Then Annie, who we all call "Awesomely Awkward" for a reason, said in her loving yet mocking and horrifyingly loud voice: "Oh my god, you guys are adorable, become a couple RIGHT now."

THEN (MOST HORRIFYING OF ALL)

Mari told me later that she hadn't known what was going on, but everything got quiet and she wondered what had happened. We laughed awkwardly—that's what happened. And I felt like I was basically gonna black out. Then Sam said something like, "It's a bit soon for that," which finally broke the tension, and everyone laughed. I have to say it made me happy that he didn't deny it. Not that he confirmed it, but he didn't deny we were a couple.

Come time to go, we sat up, and he rubbed my back in a disturbingly fatherly manner then leaned in a bit like he was going to kiss me but didn't. Then he gave me a long hug. I think he would have kissed me if there hadn't been so many people watching us. But today at school we barely talked. And the happiness has been enveloped by worry. Should we hang out separate from the group now? We've never done that before, except for when we're backstage. But being on our own would probably make it less awkward to cuddle, or maybe MORE awkward? Should we go on a date or to prom? (He's a junior after all.) Or since we've held hands should we hold hands at school or in public? What if this turns into nothing and totally fizzles just like things did with Owen? And scarier, what if it really turns into something?

Because I have a funny and frightening feeling it just might. And I have no fucking idea what I'm doing.

TUESDAY, NOVEMBER 14, ? P.M.

Wow. A LOT has happened since I last wrote. I don't even know where to start. Firstly, it has been ridiculously stormy and all of South Hill's power is out. So, I'm lying in bed writing this with a headlamp.

Secondly, Sam and I are "together," which means that more cuddling has occurred....He came over yesterday and well...we kind of...made out in my room.

YES.

I suppose I should go back to Nora's movie night, which was last Friday. We all watched *Clue*, and Nora kept getting mad when people would laugh and comment on the movie. She'd say, "Shhh!!" but then quote along with it herself and do all the accents. I have to say I wasn't really paying much attention to the movie....Sam and I were sharing a blanket, and held hands and kept each other warm and he even kissed my hand once. It went on all night. And I felt like my head was in a cloud and like everything around us was in black and white.

Something mortifying DID happen, though, which thankfully didn't change anything with Sam. Because for a second I thought everything was done for.

I had gotten up to pee during the movie, but once I got to the bathroom I realized my period had come.

I couldn't find any pads or tampons in Nora's bathroom, so I stealthily crept back out to grab one from my purse. But, Nora's bathroom is kind of in the middle of the house, with a door on each side. I had gone out one door, into her room to look for my purse, and when I turned around, that door was locked, because someone had

SHIT.

come in from the kitchen side!!! I thought I'd only be gone for a second—I had left the toilet. Full of paper. And pee. And BLOOD.

I wanted to DIE. Especially because when the door opened back up, out walked SAM.

He just smiled and I ran in like a silent mouse and dealt with my period as quickly as I could before returning to the group and my spot by his side.

I cannot believe the gory mess he must have seen. With god as my witness, I hereby vow to never leave a toilet unflushed again.

When the night was over, he still only gave me a hug again. We need to find some time alone!!! We're always with the group. And it's starting to feel like we should talk about "us." I think both of us were avoiding having the "Are we a couple?" conversation, but it's just starting to feel more and more apropos.

But then, yesterday, we walked to my house after school. It started to rain right when we got to my alley, so we had to run to the house to avoid getting wet.

It's starting to get really cold and blustery outside, and all the leaves have fallen off the trees. It was so cozy inside, and we had tea and gingerbread that Mom had baked the night before (so quaint, I know).

We were all alone, since Mom and Dad don't get home till evening. And after we ate, we went upstairs and lay on my bed and just cuddled, like we often do when we're hanging out with other friends, but this time it felt so much more momentous and clearer that something was really going on, since we were alone. He reached out and held my hand. And when he touched me it sent shivers down my spine. I felt like a skeleton being electrocuted in a cartoon.

He kept touching my temples and hair, and then he kissed my forehead. Then both cheeks, and my forehead, and repeated the pattern over and over, making a triangle. And then…finally, we kissed. On the lips.

We kissed and kissed for I don't even know how long. It could have been a lifetime—it was like I melted into him. We just lay with our arms around each other kissing and melting, and I can't even describe it. It was kind of like I imagined, only slightly more awkward? But also slightly less. I've always worried that I wouldn't know how to kiss when the time came. But it was like my body knew what to do, like we were

moving in sync, as one being. And although I didn't worry at the time, now I'm worrying about how bad I was since it was my first time, and I know it wasn't his.

We still didn't talk about "us."...But now...I assume we're together...?

I want to sleep now, but I'll write soon.
 Love, P

WEDNESDAY, DECEMBER 13, 10:17 P.M.

It would be impossible to write down everything that has happened every day in the month I haven't written. Everything would be a montage of different adjectives, all trying in vain to describe the roller coaster of emotions that have occurred.

In middle school I took art classes from a woman named Joy Penfold. I didn't like her much, or her classes (we only painted boring still lifes and animals from photos), but once I remember another student asked her how you can tell when your painting is done. And she said,

PAINT UNTIL EVERYTHING STARTS TO MELT INTO one Beautiful whole.

And I liked that. That's what it's been like. With Sam. Like everything is swirling into a glorious vortex of glowing warmth. Like I'm just slipping further and further into an abyss of sweetness and softness and love, and the deeper I sink, the more I forget what my life was even like before Sam.

So much has happened since our first kiss.

We hang out often after school, unless he has to study. I usually hang out with Mari and Nora on those days and catch them up on the gossip, or have an afternoon to myself where I either paint or just gaze out the window thinking about Sam.

Our routine is dialed in—meet at the Little Theater after school and walk to my house. I feel bad because Asher is always offering me rides, but all I want to do is walk with Sam.

Once home, it's herbal tea, talking, and maybe a game of Skip-Bo or Uno, then it's up to my room or on to the couch for kissing...and touching...and more.

Because yes...there's been more.

It was about the third or fourth time we made out in my room that he put his hand up my shirt.

And then the next time, both our shirts and my bra came completely off. And I can't even describe the buttery softness of what it felt like for our skin to touch.

It felt like magic. So silky and warm. It was like when you touch a rabbit's ear, or a cat's paw, and your body can't even comprehend the softness.

On weekends we usually hang out at his house. It's farther away from school, so it's not as good of a walking destination, but on Saturday nights I can persuade Mom and Dad to drive me there and pick me up again late at night.

Last Saturday, while his mom was making dinner, we went and walked around his neighborhood in the frosty, biting cold. We lay on his trampoline and looked up at the stars and kissed and kissed. His hands were so cold against my skin when they went up my shirt, but I didn't mind. Then, we unzipped each other's flies and I put my hand down his pants and he put his down mine.

I THINK maybe I had my first orgasm there, under the night sky, on Sam's trampoline. He had one, that's for sure. He finished first, and I kind of clenched my butt for a really long time while he fingered me,  until I couldn't for one second longer. And then when I relaxed, I felt a warm trembly feeling in my muscles, like when you sprint for a few minutes and your heart is beating fast and you feel kind of elated like you're going to hysterically laugh or cry. So, I think maybe that was it...?

After the trampoline, we had to go inside for dinner. It felt bright and alien and we had to try to be normal around his family, and I kept worrying that they'd heard us or would somehow know what we had been doing outside. His mom made lentils and brown rice, which was bland and saltless and everything was vegetarian, and I felt like I shouldn't eat very much or salt my food because all their portions were so small and they seemed so content without any seasoning, so I didn't want to be the rogue salt fiend at the table, or even ask for more.

After dinner his little sister, Linnea, just wanted to show me the drawings she'd made at Waldorf school. I think it's kind of weird that at Waldorf school you're not allowed to draw whatever you want, that you can only paint and use certain materials at certain times. It just seems so intense and strict. I definitely never could have abided by those rules. I hate how little control you have with wet-on-wet watercolors and it seems like that's all they can do. Or pastels, which I also hate. Like why stop kids from being able to make whatever they want?

After that we watched *Jeopardy!* with his parents and all of them knew all the answers and shouted them out. Sam said his mom auditioned for *Jeopardy!* once, and made it to the final round, but didn't get cast because they said she "wasn't enough of a personality." I would never have guessed that is one of their criteria based on watching the show, since it seems like no personality is almost a prerequisite.

I like Sam's family but I'm definitely a little intimidated by his parents, who I feel like secretly think I'm not good enough for Sam. That they think he should be with someone more intellectual and less whimsical or something.

Friday, December 15, 10:25 p.m.

Tonight I went to a play at the iDiOM Theater with the drama crew. The iDiOM is a tiny, amazing theater behind the Pickford cinema downtown. Ms. Hanley is giving us extra credit for any plays we see, so it was a perfect excuse to go, especially because they were doing short plays based on the books of Edward Gorey, who Dad and I love. None of my friends had ever even heard of him before.

I went with Mari, Nora, David, and Sam, which has been the regular crew of late.

We have been going on lots of double-ish dates now that Sam and I are together, and David and Mari have also been a thing since the infamous Halloween party hookup. But of course Nora comes too, as the fifth wheel, which I don't think she minds, but she is hard to read sometimes. I definitely wish she'd catch a hint and let us go do couples-y things on our own occasionally.

It was hard at first telling her about Sam and me, since I knew she liked him too. I waited too long.

Until well after we'd kissed. I know I should have talked to her about it after we held hands and cuddled at her movie night. I think she knew, because she'd seen those things, and I was worried she'd be mad that I'd waited so long to bring it up.

I was at her house, and we'd stayed up late hypothesizing about the next (and last) Harry Potter book (which comes out THIS SUMMER) and planning our costumes for the release. Then I just kind of blurted it out.

She was just quiet at first, which is why I thought she was mad.

And I felt bad. Because she also had never been kissed or had a boy-friend, so for some reason, I felt bad that I had moved ahead, like I was leaving her behind. But it's not like I shouldn't have done it until the time was right for Nora to kiss someone too—it's not like I'm supposed to wait around and not live my life until she can be kissed alongside me at the exact same time....I shouldn't have to feel bad. Sam and I HAP-PENED to fall in love. It wasn't even something I necessarily CHOSE.

Anyway, finally she said, "I SAY!" in a dramatic British accent, pretend-ing to be surprised. And I could tell if she WAS upset, she wasn't going to show it. So I just moved on, and told her about everything we'd been doing, and how amazing it's been, and she kept reacting in that gushy, fake, theatrical way, throwing her head back and laughing.

It just felt so weird. Like she hadn't known what to say, and so put on a show instead.

Anyway. The Edward Gorey play was sooooooo cool. When we walked into the theater, a live band was playing eerie music on an accordion and musical saw!! We were all dressed up in our "going-to-the-theater" best. That is, as "best" as is possible in Bellingham without looking like you're in a play yourself, since most people here consider a Life is Good T-shirt with Birkenstocks to be "dressed up." Sam looked so cute in a tweed sport coat and tie (although it was a little wide), and David wore a silk scarf. During the intermission, we went out and stood in the cold, and I wished Sam would wrap his arms around me to keep me warm or give me his coat like David had to Mari, but he's so cautious about PDA that he didn't initiate it and I was too shy to ask. Plus his coat probably wouldn't have fit me anyway, so it's probably better we were spared that situation. He DID hold my hand in the theater, though, when the lights went out. It was so warm and felt so lovely and soft. I tried to focus on how nice it felt instead of how uncomfortably narrow the wooden theater seats were.

The actors in the play were SO cool. Everyone in the show wore only black and gray and white, like they were in an Edward Gorey illustration, and had dark eyeliner around their eyes.

There was one lady in the play who I couldn't take my eyes off of. There was something about her that made my heart hurt.

I wasn't even sure why at first. It was like when I see a piece of art I love so much that it feels almost lonely to know that no one will ever understand how powerfully it speaks to you.

Her body looked like mine.

And it's not like I've never seen someone like that before. But she was different. She was so...out there, and hip, and happy seeming. And beautiful.

After the show she was standing outside with the other actors, laughing and smoking, still in their costumes and being hip.

I wanted to linger outside to watch her more, to try to say hi and tell her that she did a good job. But everyone else was cold, so we left and sought refuge inside Fantasia café for London Fogs.

I saved the program from the play, and the next day I looked her up on Myspace, like a creep!!!! Her name is Olivia Wormwood. Even her name is cool!!!

She had lots of amazing pictures in cool outfits and big sunglasses, and even one of her in a vintage-y swimsuit, and I really want to know where she got it.

I felt like a complete stalker, but I went back to her Myspace again today. She seems sooo cool. I keep making up stories about her in my head.

I IMAGINE SHE LIVES IN A BEAUTIFUL, CHIC APARTMENT WITH WALLPAPER LIKE IN "AMÉLIE" AND PROBABLY HAS A BLACK CAT.

Saturday, December 16, 7:31 p.m.

It's the second night of Hanukkah tonight. I hate holidays because everyone is stressed and when my family is stressed, they pick on me. Today at breakfast I reached for the last piece of bacon and Dad said, "Cool it on the bacon, P. You've already had three pieces."

I can't wait for Roxie to come home so she can defend me from Mom and Dad. When I was little Mom wouldn't let me eat snacks after dinner, and once Roxie yelled at Mom, "If she's hungry, she should eat!" and snuck food to me in my room.

Although, to be fair, she probably called me Dudley Dursley or Fat Lard the next day.

Today I went to the antique store to buy Nora a birthday present. I stole $20 worth of jewelry and then felt guilty so I paid for an old photograph of a child long dead who I don't know. Plus I bought Nora a flowered tin and some vintage lacy handkerchiefs.

NORA'S PRESENTS

SHAMEFUL (BUT COOL...) TREASURES

I feel in a melancholy mood.

And my shoes need laces.

And my eyes are stinging from the onions in the latkes that Mom is making.

And my garbage needs taking out.

And I don't know the basic Hebrew prayer.

And Sam's cum is on my sheets, but I still haven't washed them because I'm afraid Mom will somehow see.

And I'm in love. And I want to cry and scream and laugh like I'm in some crap romance movie with Jennifer Garner.

Friday, December 22, 12:45 p.m.

We are on winter break! I can't believe the year is halfway done.

I'm excited for a break but also sad because I've been loving my classes and hanging out with friends at school. On Wednesday, which was the last day, I gave Ms. Hanley a little painting I made of her and her husband for Christmas, and she was so excited she put it up at her desk.

In Yearbook, Asher Wilson and I edited photos in the workroom together, and then after class he gave me a mix CD.

I felt bad because I didn't have anything for him. I should try to remember to make him a mix while I'm on break, even though I feel like he already knows and has all the songs I'd put on it.

Here's what's on the one he made me:

1. *The Purple Bottle, Animal Collective*
2. *Girl from the North Country, Bob Dylan*
3. *Anyone Else but You, The Moldy Peaches*
4. *Snow Owl, The Mountain Goats*
5. *Do You Realize??, The Flaming Lips*
6. *God Only Knows, The Beach Boys*
7. *First Day of My Life, Bright Eyes*
8. *Everyday, Buddy Holly*
9. *Lived In Bars, Cat Power*
10. *The New Year, Death Cab for Cutie*

After school got out, Sam and Nora and I went over to Mari's and ended up hanging out for over 24 hours there! We had so much fun.

It had snowed the day before and we all played in the snow for hours and hours, sledding down the big hill on saucers and old sleds we dug out from under the house.

Then we went inside all wet, cold, and happy and baked cookies.

We drank tea and played Balderdash and Scattergories under blankets all day long. Mari's family has a real woodstove, which her dad lit for us in the evening. Then the rest of the crew came too—David, Annie, Jenna, and even Lukas and Owen, who have been a little more enigmatic lately since *Tom Jones* ended. I bet Lukas came because we were hanging out at Mari's house. And even though Mari seems convinced that he doesn't like her, I feel like their magnetic pull is too much for him to resist. It's not like he comes to the hangouts we have at

Nora's. Mari's parents made us lasagna for dinner, and then it started snowing some more! After dinner we watched Mari's and my childhood favorite—the old 80s BBC version of *The Lion, the Witch and the Wardrobe*. No one else had ever seen it, which scandalized Mari and me! We were all piled around on couches and cuddled under blankets. I love that I have friends who are interested in partaking in such nostalgic cozy weirdness.

I kept wondering if Owen was noticing Sam and me stealing kisses and holding hands. This was really the first time he'd been around everyone in a while, since Sam and I have been "official." I kept trying to sneak glances at him to see if he looked jealous, but I couldn't tell. He was just normal, happy-go-lucky Owen and didn't really even seem to notice that Sam and I are together now, which annoyed me, even though I know I shouldn't care about him anymore. I can't believe kissing is just normal for me now. And more than kissing even. If you would have told my year-ago self that by this time I would have lost track of all the kisses I've received, and hand jobs I've given, I would have been over the moon.

Everyone except Owen slept over (he had ballet in the morning), the boys in the living room and the girls packed into Mari's bed and on her floor. I could barely sleep all night thinking about how close by Sam was sleeping, just a few footsteps away in the other room. If I would have been bolder, I might have padded out and slipped under the blanket with him in the middle of the night, but I was too worried about being caught by Mari's mom, who is friends with my mom, and ruining any chances of future coed sleepovers, which all our parents only said was okay if the boys and girls slept in different rooms, no exceptions.

My heart was beating SO fast while I was trying to get to sleep, and I was only half listening to the conversations Nora, Mari, Jenna, and Annie were having until late at night. I wondered if Mari felt the same way about David sleeping so close. It's hard to tell how she feels about him still, even though she says she likes him. I think she does, but I don't get the sense that it's love. More of a "why not" kind of thing, and I definitely saw her flirting with Lukas whenever David wasn't around tonight.

In the morning we helped Lukas dig his old silver Saab out of Mari's driveway so he could heroically drive to get us doughnuts from LaFeen's. When he got back we had them with big mugs of milky black tea and looked out the windows at the snow. It was so fun to see everyone, and especially the boys' tousled bedhead and groggy morning faces. They all looked so cute, somehow younger and more innocent than usual. The snow made it feel like we were all holed up in a ski lodge or snowed in at a British manor house, like in the Miss Marple mysteries I like to watch with Mom.

After breakfast, still in pajamas, we played

THE QUESTIONS

Mari had learned The Questions from the other teens at the new age singing camp she goes to with her family and said she had been waiting since summer for the right time to play it with all of us. Basically, you just ask a series of questions and don't tell people until later what their answers symbolize.

The questions are:

1) You're standing on the edge of a cliff. Describe what everything around you looks like, and how you feel.
2) You're inside an empty room with no windows and no doors. Describe it, and how it makes you feel.
3) If you were an animal, what would you be?
4) What is an animal you admire but wouldn't want to be?
5) If you were a body of water, what would you be and why?

Mari went first, because she'd played before and had her answers ready as an example.

Her cliff looked like the Grand Canyon, rocky and dry, and she felt scared at first but eventually sat down and appreciated the beauty.

She said she definitely felt panicky in the white room and would be overthinking being there and what she was going to do. For number three, she said cat, because they're relaxed and playful but slightly aloof. For four: a dog, because they're enthusiastic and loyal and gregarious. For water, she said she'd be a peaceful inlet, surrounded by trees, with waves lapping gently at the shore.

I was second to go.

For question one, I imagined a beautiful, rugged sea cliff with birds wheeling in the distance and salty sea wind blowing my hair around. The sky was big and open and full of blue-gray clouds. I felt exhilarated, and a little scared, but not in a bad way. Mostly overwhelmed, and excited about all there was to see and feel. I think I was picturing Washington Park, in Anacortes, where I went with my dad when I was a kid.

For two, I said at first I felt claustrophobic, but that eventually a feeling of resignation and peace washed over me, and I just surrendered to the blank, inescapable-ness of it all.

For the animal I wasn't sure what to say. I'm always torn between an owl and a swimming mammal like an otter or a seal. I went with otter, because they're happy and cute, and because I love to swim. For the animal I admire, I said a cat, because they seem wise and deep-thinking. To be honest, I mostly just said it because I guessed Sam was going to say cat for his animal he identified with, because I know he likes them, and Mari already told me privately that that question represents "what you look for in a mate." So I kind of cheated. But it's not like I don't REALLY think that about cats.

For the body of water I said a river. I've always loved swimming in rivers. I love how fresh and active they are, how it feels to have your flesh and hair pushed at and rippled. I love feeling the constant, roiling strength of the water, but how there are also pools and eddies that are calm and serene.

Most people's cliff and room responses were variations on Mari's and mine, either sea or Grand-Canyon-y cliffs, usually feeling exhilarated and overwhelmed, and then all-black or all-white rooms and feeling trapped or meditative.

For water, he said he'd be a bubbling alpine brook, because he loves the sound of them when he's backpacking with his family in the mountains, that they feel playful yet "ensure an abundance of resources." (SO Sam.)

Once we all gave our answers, Mari told us what they meant.

THE **CLIFF** IS HOW YOU FEEL ABOUT <u>LIFE</u>. THE **ROOM** IS HOW YOU FEEL ABOUT <u>DEATH</u>. YOUR ANIMAL IS HOW YOU SEE <u>YOURSELF</u>, THE ANIMAL YOU ADMIRE IS WHAT YOU'RE <u>ATTRACTED TO</u>... AND THE BODY OF WATER IS HOW YOU FEEL ABOUT **SEX**!!!

ANNIE'S BONG WATER!

It couldn't be more apropos of course. But I saw her give me a hurt look and then sneak off to the bathroom when the subject was changed. And now I feel bad. Why can't she just play along like Annie? Annie's answer wasn't exactly flattering either, but at least she can take a joke.

After The Questions we all went and played in the snow again, then once we came back in people slowly started to head home. We'd been hanging out for so long! Sam and I stayed the latest, till it was just him, Mari, and me. I wished it didn't have to end. I knew home was going to be boring in comparison to being so cozy with my friends.

It was dark when Sam walked me down the trail to my house, he was going down the street to catch the bus home. But first, we paused in the snow. It was up to our knees, with a hard layer of ice on top, and glowing blue in the darkness. Flakes had stopped falling, the night sky was velvety black, and you could see the stars perfectly clear. We craned our necks to look up at them, and when I lowered my head, Sam was looking at me, smiling. "I wish we didn't have to stop hanging out," he said. "Me too," I said.

We huddled for warmth, taking a moment to hold each other tight under the giant frozen sky. We kissed and kissed, our bodies keeping us warm and our breath rising into soft clouds that were bright white in the dark night.

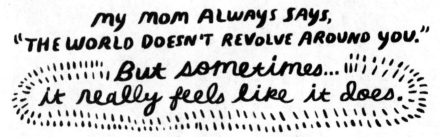

my mom ALWAYS SAYS, "THE WORLD DOESN'T REVOLVE AROUND YOU." But sometimes... it really feels like it does.

SATURDAY, DECEMBER 23, 10:49 P.M.

We had our annual Hanukkah dinner with Mari's family last night, but this was the first year in a long time that Mari and I are friends again, so it was actually fun! Auntie Eve, Mom's sister, is visiting all the way from Florida.

AUNTIE EVE

ALWAYS READY WITH A FOLK SONG

♪ SOMOS EL BAAARCO...

CLASSIC BUSHY HAIR

BATIK GARMENT OF SOME KIND

SPACED-OUT, MELLOW EXPRESSION

LOTS OF AMBER & TURQUOISE JEWELRY

We waited until the last night of Hanukkah to have our big dinner so that she and Roxie would both be here. I kinda wish we would have done it without Roxie, though, because I feel like she made things weird now that Mari and I are friends again. Before the Blumes came over she kept saying things like, "I can't believe you're friends with someone who wears 'butt-less' jeans." Which is what we call jeans that don't have any back pockets. It makes me worry that I'm doing something wrong by being friends with Mari again, if Roxie still thinks she's that uncool. But she and I have so much fun together, and it's been so nice having a girl-friend again who lives so close. I always feel so happy and FULL after we hang out. I'm just so tired of Roxie making me feel like nothing I do is good enough or cool enough for her. I wish I didn't care so much about what she thinks. She doesn't even live here anymore, yet every time she waltzes in, I start to second-guess my friendships and relationships that I know deep down are so good. I can just see the judgment on her face. She acted too cool all night at dinner. She pretended not to know how to play dreidel, even though she's always been the one who knew the rules, and didn't sing along with the prayers when we lit the candles.

231

Dad made a zany menorah this year out of a branch from the yard, because Mom couldn't find her favorite silver one. He painted it red and yellow and blue and melted candles onto nine of the branch tips.

Mom is always extra frazzled and annoyed when she's cooking for groups. And when Auntie Eve visits. Auntie Eve is ten years older than Mom and is Mom's only living family member (her brother died when I was six and her parents when I was nine). There's always so much anticipation around her visits, but then it feels like the whole time she's here Mom is annoyed at her for going off and meditating all the time.

Anyway. Surprise, surprise, Dad's homemade menorah caught on fire and all of us laughed so hard, even Mom, and the smoke alarm went off AGAIN. Roxie didn't laugh. She said, "What did you think would happen?" and just rolled her eyes and went off to text one of her friends. She can be such a bitch. It was so funny! And Dad was walking around for the rest of the night with a singed beard.

Then after dinner, after everyone had left, Roxie got into some big fight with Mom. I don't even remember what it was about, and Mom said that Roxie had been "grouchy all evening."

Roxie said, "It's hard not to be grouchy when we're having dinner with people who hate me. The Blumes only like Phoebe—they hate me because I'm not good at art and I don't do drama with their precious Mari!" Mom said, "You're being ridiculous, honey. They don't hate you." But I was feeling so annoyed at her that I had to pipe up.

THEY DON'T HATE YOU BECAUSE YOU DON'T DO DRAMA, THEY HATE YOU BECAUSE YOU ACT LIKE A BITCH.

Roxie went upstairs, mad.

But it's true.

She's always saying people aren't friendly to her, but I don't think she realizes how cold she can come off, and so maybe people just give up being friendly after a while.

Anyway. She eventually came downstairs, and we had our annual viewing of *A Muppet Family Christmas* that our neighbor recorded off TV on a VHS in 1989. All the old commercials are on it and we have them memorized. We ate satsumas nonstop, and everything was fine. Maybe Auntie Eve did some Reiki on Roxie while she was upstairs and that calmed her down.

WATCH THE ICY PATCH!

TUESDAY, DECEMBER 26, 1:15 P.M.

Christmas was good. We kept strictly to tradition—I woke Roxie up early by crawling into her bed, then we roused Mom and Dad. Mom tried to say we had to wait for Auntie Eve to wake up before we could start presents, and Roxie and I just about rioted because we knew that wouldn't be for hours. We decided to let her sleep, though, and went downstairs to unwrap stocking presents first. Then we made sourdough waffles with applesauce and Mom's homemade raspberry jam and bacon. Finally, after we'd dragged out the breakfast process for what felt like 17 years, Auntie Eve emerged from her room and said, "Good morning" in her calm, spacey way that did not at ALL acknowledge the urgency and excitement that is Christmas morning!!!!

After presents Dad, who was wearing a fuzzy Santa hat and whistling, gathered up all the crumpled wrapping paper that had been strewn around the living room before we went over to Grandma and Grandpa's for a while. Auntie Eve conveniently went upstairs to "rest and meditate" instead of helping with breakfast cleanup. I put on my new robe and wished I could see Sam and give him a Christmas kiss, although since his family is more Jew-y than mine and therefore doesn't celebrate, I guess it wouldn't be a Christmas kiss for him. But it would still

XMAS
Present Inventory

- **CDS FROM ROXIE**
  (RATATAT, KINGS OF CONVENIENCE, BEN FOLDS)

- **VINTAGE PINK WOOL ROBE FROM MOM**
  (WHICH MAKES ME FEEL LIKE AN OLDEN-DAYS
  HOLLYWOOD STARLET.)

- **STAR HEADBAND ROXIE MADE**

- **GOLD CLUTCH**

- **OLD POLAROID FROM DAD**

- **DVDs FROM AUNTIE EVE**
  MONTY PYTHON & "NAPOLEON DYNAMITE."
  SHE MUST HAVE ASKED MOM FOR TIPS!)

- **BOOKS, ART SUPPLIES & STOCKING STUFFERS**
  (INCLUDING THE TRADITIONAL CANNED, SMOKED OYSTERS
  WE ALWAYS GET FROM DAD.)

be special. For Hanukkah he gave me *White Teeth* by Zadie Smith, one of his favorite books. I gave him a red wool scarf that I had embroidered a tiny heart onto. I unoriginally got the idea from the Gossip Girl books (one of the characters embroiders a little heart on her boyfriend's sleeve).

He's so bad at texting. I asked him earlier what he was doing today, and he still hasn't written back. He's going on a ski trip to Utah with his family tomorrow and I want to see him before he leaves. Gotta go. I am being forced into a family folk song session at the piano by Mom and Auntie Eve, who seems to have brought her dulcimer all the way from Florida.

4:16 P.M.

I'm feeling a bit listless.

It's that day-after-Christmas feeling of emptiness. Mom keeps suggesting we go on a walk and it's pissing me off. She's obsessed with walking!

She should get Auntie Eve to go!! But I know Mom doesn't want to ask her because every time they go on walks Auntie Eve insists on bringing her divining rods and goes too slow for Mom's all-business pace.

Mari is out of town with her family today, so I can't run up the trail to her house and gossip about our lovers like we have been almost every day of break so far. We've been taking neighborhood walks so we can talk about sex without our parents hearing. Not that I think her mom would really care. Everyone says Mari has had sex with Lukas, and that that's what's at the root of the romantic tension that everyone knows is between them. But she says they haven't, and that people just like to make things up. That the one time they did hook up last year, all they did was make out in his Saab at the beach. And that the furthest she's gone has been a BJ with David this year. She said she's tired of everyone pairing her and Lukas up, that she liked him but it doesn't seem like he likes her and that she feels like there is so much pressure because they almost always get cast as the romantic leads (except for in *Tom Jones*, when it was her and David).

I don't feel like I can talk to Roxie about sex. I tried to last night and she just lectured me about how I should wait, because she did until she was 19. She said she never wanted to do it before that, and so I shouldn't either. And I can't talk to Nora about it because I just know she can't relate. She gets so awkward and shuts down every time I bring it up. Maybe because she liked Sam too, but that was so long ago. I think she's just a prude. She doesn't know "how far" we've gotten, and Roxie doesn't either. But Mari does, and she doesn't make me feel bad about it.

I'm not afraid of sex. I'm excited. Because when Sam and I are together, I always want more. I've always thought I wouldn't wait long to
do it once I was in a relationship. Although sometimes I do wonder if
I'm going too fast. I think about how just two months ago I'd never even
been kissed. And how that first time we held hands—that electricity was
enough to keep me high for a week. Then we kissed, and touched, and
touched some more. And how when we started it was like we were trying
to devour each other, then we found delicacy, bringing a stronger and
more tender passion. And now, the next step is…sex, I think.

WEDNESDAY, DECEMBER 27, 9:29 P.M.

I'm alternating, chocolate, ChapStick, chocolate, ChapStick. Waiting for Sam to come home from his ski trip.

But he only left this morning, so I still have seven days. Seven days of Roxie telling me that I'm not really feeling what I'm feeling for Sam, that I'm just being impulsive and naive. And all I told her was that I was thinking about having sex. Just THINKING about it. And she freaked out.

Her telling me not to just makes me want to do it more. I want to prove to her and everyone else that I'm not the annoying kid sister anymore. That I'm mature and know what I want. But it's impossible, because I will always be the kid sister to her, the one who everyone makes fun of. If I have sex with Sam and I tell Roxie, she will think I'm doing it just to prove that I'm not the kid sister. Which I guess I just said that I am.... But that isn't really what it's ALL about.

I really DO just WANT to do it. I want to know what it's like. I keep thinking about him. I keep wondering where it will be, and how it will feel.

THURSDAY, DECEMBER 28, ? P.M.

I'm sitting on the frozen ground at the park, at the little lookout spot where Sam and I once stood on one of our early dates in November and watched the salmon try to get upstream. Roxie and I got into a fight. It was because we were making these little heart pins out of felt and fabric that said "I heart you" in cursive.

I wanted the simpler, less decorated one, which I liked more. And Roxie accused me of taking the "better" one, and it spurred a CLASSIC "You're a selfish, lazy bitch" argument.

Which somehow turned into me CRYING and telling her everything I've been wanting to lately about how much I can't STAND her, and that continued as we got into the car to go pick up Mom from choir practice.

Roxie thinks she's SO much cooler and wiser than me because she's four years older and lives on her own in Seattle. We hadn't even gotten down the driveway before she kicked me out of the car. I didn't feel like going back home, so I walked and walked and I came here because I miss Sam so much. And my butt is numb from sitting on the cold gravel. But I'm not going to go home.

MONDAY, JANUARY 1, 2:44 P.M.

My 16th birthday is in exactly 23 days!!!

Last night for New Year's we got together with the Blumes and Mari and I hung out while our parents played Scrabble all night. Roxie is back in Seattle with her friends, so it was funner without her grouchiness around. I wish Sam could have come, but he's still skiing in Utah. Sigh.

Mom made chocolate babka and we all drank Martinelli's sparkling cider and went out on the porch to bang on pots and pans with wooden spoons when midnight came.

I wish I could have kissed Sam right at 12. I called him at 12:05, but no luck. When I got in bed my phone buzzed and I got excited that it was Sam. Instead I had New Year's texts from Roxie and Annie, and one from Asher Wilson that said, "Happy Newt Year. Check track 10 of my mix." Which is "The New Year" by Death Cab. I spent an ungodly amount of time trying to think of an en-theme song idea to send him back but fell asleep before I could. When I woke up the next morning, lo and behold, I had a voice mail from Sam that came in at 1:30 a.m.!!!! I could have cried with happiness and relief. I could tell he was talking quietly, because his family was asleep, and just his voice made me melt.

Even though it was perfectly sweet I couldn't help but feel disappointed that he hadn't said more. That he hadn't said "I love you" or "I wish I was there."

P.S.

I think if I told Dad that Sam didn't know who Neil Young was, he'd disown me and make me break up with him on the spot.

Sunday, January 7, 6:20 p.m.

I'm excited to be back at school this week. There were parts of winter break that were really fun, but I miss seeing Sam and the rest of the drama crew! I had thought we'd have lots of time during break to hang out, but he was always off having to do things with family and so was I.

My classes this semester are much the same as the last one, with the exception of art, which is new. I have Yearbook, Drama 3 (part 2), French 3 (part 2), and Studio Art. I wanted to take a semester off doing French because I didn't want to take four classes, but Mom was worried that I'd lose all of it if I don't take it again. I'm still doing the part-time home-schooler thing because I just can't be bothered to take "real" classes when it's so much nicer to have a loose schedule. I'm nervous to take Studio Art, because even though I know I'm "good," I've never taken an art class in high school, and I'm worried that I won't be able to do whatever I want. I had to apply to get in as a sophomore, because I haven't taken Art 1 & 2, which are usually required. I had to have a portfolio review with the teacher, Mr. Schmidt, in his classroom and show him a bunch of my artwork and talk about why it was important to me to be able to do a studio-style class when I can make up my own curriculum.

I was really intimidated by him at first because he's kind of New York–y and brusque and intense, and the art room is so cool. There are tons of pottery wheels and big tables for people to do drawings and make things out of clay, and he has a bunch of amazing art books you can borrow, and so many supplies. When I walk in there I get this excited feeling that I can barely explain—it's almost like when you see a crush and have kind of a knot in your chest, but mixed with this intense yearning to make all the things I want to make, all at once. I thought Mr. Schmidt was

going to be really harsh with me about how I wanted to skip the prerequisites, but he just said, "Okie-doke, well, it definitely seems like you know what you're doing," and I said I did. He seems very cool.

Yearbook of course is always year-round, and so it was back to the usual grind of photo taking and caption writing and making layouts and goofing off with Asher in class.

I made a CD to give to him tomorrow in return for the one he gave me, which was SO good! Here's what's on his:

1. *This Time Tomorrow, The Kinks*
2. *It's a Hit, Rilo Kiley*
3. *Our House, Phantom Planet*
4. *Hear Me Out, Ben Kweller*

5. The Mistress Witch from McClure (Or the Mind That Knows Itself), Sufjan Stevens
6. Ceremony, New Order
7. 100,000 Fireflies, The Magnetic Fields
8. Magnetized, Laura Veirs
9. Get Me Away from Here, I'm Dying, Belle and Sebastian
10. I'll Be Your Mirror, The Velvet Underground

TUESDAY, JANUARY 9, 8:31 P.M.

Today Sam and I talked. Not just talked but..."talked."

He came over after school, in our usual tradition, and we chatted and played Skip-Bo and stayed inside, out of the rain and wind. Then we kissed and kissed and then my mouth was filled with the smooth and salty taste of his dick. Kisses of gratitude, and then it was over.

And then I said it. I whispered it.

SILENCE.

THEN HE SAID MY NAME.
AND THAT SCARED ME, BECAUSE
I REALIZED HOW SERIOUS WHAT
I'D JUST SAID WAS.

251

OH, PHOEBE... I DON'T KNOW...

It was barely audible.

And we talked about it. And I think it honestly hadn't crossed his mind. And I felt horrible, like I was pressuring him by even just bringing it up. I felt like some kind of slut that it had even been on my mind. I have just...been wanting so bad to say it out loud because some days it feels like it's just hovering there, between us, like an exciting question mark, and I wanted to know if he thought about it too, or if I was some kind of floozy freak thinking too far ahead.

He kept trying to speak and couldn't, and when he did, it sounded like he was about to cry. And seeing him unsure made me feel unsure. It made me want to cry and apologize and act like I'd never said anything. He said something about how he wasn't very experienced. I told him I wasn't either, he knows that. Then he said something about how we'd only been together two months. And that he tended to be on the more prudish side of things, which made me feel slutty. But he concurred that we weren't THAT young.

Then he said that the other day he was in the car with his dad and out of the blue his dad said, "I don't think you should have sex with Phoebe," and that was the first time he had really thought about it at all. How is that possible? Aren't teenage boys supposed to be the horny ones, yet here I am obsessing ever since I can remember about when and how this moment of my life would come, and he's some puritan baby angel being influenced by his randomly scheming father? And why doesn't his dad think we should have sex? Not that most parents would jump for joy at the idea, but would he say that about any girlfriend of Sam's, or does he think I'm some especially wayward temptress?

I just can't help but be pissed off that his dad bringing it up was the first time he'd ever even THOUGHT about the concept at all.

Ugh. I know there isn't anything to do but sit and wait to see what the future holds.

10:50 *p.m.*

I can't get the moment he said my name out of my head. "Oh, Phoebe..."

Like he was scared and exasperated and couldn't find any words. Him saying my name almost felt like I was being pulled from a dream world, where our thoughts and actions were in sync. I was all done being afraid of sex, all done being afraid that I shouldn't want what I want. I convinced myself that this was something more than just a high school relationship. My first boyfriend. And maybe Sam thinks it's just a petty, high school few-months deal.

He was so adorably afraid of saying it. I wanted to burst into tears. I read on a horoscope website that Virgo and Aquarius's biggest problem is communication, that I'm going to have to work at it. Communicate, communicate, communicate, I tell myself when I'm around him.

And I love him. And now I'm afraid he doesn't love me. Because if he did, wouldn't he have said yes? Maybe he'll break up with me because he's not ready to have sex, but I don't even know if I'm ready. I just wanted to talk about the possibility of it. We talked about how it would change our relationship. How can it not? Just having the talk changes things. Things feel so much more serious all of a sudden than they did last week. Even yesterday.

"It's not like we haven't gone far already," I said. "Yeah," he said. And then he said something about how if this is how far we've gotten in two months, what will it be like in another two? Exactly.

It would be impossible for me to describe the entire conversation. We came to no conclusion. And after he left, I felt horrible and cried. I texted him saying, "I'm sorry I inflicted awkwardness," and he wrote back saying that I shouldn't apologize, that he was glad we were comfortable enough to talk about it.

He said, "Well...some famous person once said, 'The things we regret are the things we don't do.'...But who knows, they could have been a nutcase." Which made me laugh and feel excited, like maybe he thought sex wasn't such a bad idea after all...?

God, I don't know what to write—there's too much. I want to sleep until the next time I see him. I want to cry and scream about how in love I am.

Maybe Sam is writing about it too. He writes. I write. Once he told me he was writing a play, and when I asked if I could read it he said no.

And I said, "Okay." Because I know that feeling. Showing people things you make is so exciting but sometimes it feels like some of the magic is in the private-ness, and then it gets lost when it's out in the world. But I do just want to know if he's writing about me. Or thinking about me. Sometimes I feel like when we're apart, he's just tunnel-vision doing homework and family stuff, and doesn't care about me at all until we're with each other again.

Isn't the real, and only, point of our whole existence to connect with and love other people? That sounds so easy. Why isn't it that easy?

Not even in a romantic, heart-pounding LOVE love way either, just love, like caring for someone.

Communication, communication, communication. I need to get better at it.

Do people love me? Does Sam love me? If I cannot look Sam in the eye and say "I love you" loud and clear, I cannot have sex with him.

I'm going to sleep now. It's been a long day. Good night. I love you.

Wednesday, January 10, 3:10 p.m.

I am upset and I don't know why. It's like there's something inside me fighting to get out. I shouldn't be upset; I have a boyfriend and a good life. I have at least $10 in my wallet. I keep beating myself up because I'm not an artistic genius, because at the seemingly rare time I get a brilliant idea, I can't translate it exactly and perfectly onto paper or canvas.

And it's hard to open my dresser drawers because I never fold my clothes. And because I never fold my clothes my mom lectures me, and I get annoyed. But really, I shouldn't get annoyed, because she just wants me to be more efficient. And there are dust bunnies under my bed. And I never floss my teeth. And I have a blister on my heel, and I don't want to go to school tomorrow. And my boyfriend has never told me he loves me.

And I get angry at my parents because they ask me questions, but really, I shouldn't be angry because they're just trying to make sure I'm a Good Kid. And I am a relatively Good Kid. But I feel like I should be skinnier and less selfish and should go to synagogue. And I'm sitting in my bathtub, because it just felt right. And my legs need shaving. And today I read my horoscope, because it seemed right, but I didn't relate to anything it said. And my skin is relatively clear and my hair isn't too bad. But I'm still a little bit upset.

THURSDAY, JANUARY 11, 3:45 p.m.

Today was a good day.

I woke up and saw about two inches of snow on the ground, but school wasn't canceled, which I ended up being glad about. It is wonderfully powdery wet snow too—it sits on the trees and makes you feel like you're in Narnia.

Anyway, in all my morning classes we just watched the snow.

Then during lunch I frolicked in it with Nora and Mari and David. And I saw Sam. And I almost passed out with happiness when I realized he didn't hate me after I asked about sex, and we weren't breaking up.

We all romped in the snow and took goofy photos with my new Polaroid camera. Nora took one of Sam and me that I think is the first "official" picture of us together.

We built a giant snowman with Lukas and Mari outside Principal Johnson's office, and all of these random other students came over,

S + P 1/11/07

helping or watching or taking pictures on their cell phones, and it was such a happy feeling. Working with all these people I didn't know, but it didn't matter because we were all united under one great happiness, snow. Finally, Principal Johnson herself came out and donated her very own school sweatshirt for the snowman to wear.

During Yearbook even Asher was in a good mood. Not that he's usually grumpy—just kind of in a neutral jaunty/goofy/awkward mood. But today he seemed happy. We wandered around and took pictures of the snow to document it for the yearbook. Mr. Cobb let his whole AP calc class out onto the lawn, and they were all out having a snowball fight, including Mr. Cobb himself.

For some reason I never talk about Sam with Asher, or even really think about him. It's like how we don't talk about his girlfriend, Sarah. It's a little bit like Yearbook classes with him are a weird suspended reality where it's just us and our random inside jokes and talks about music and art.

I hope school isn't canceled tomorrow. Maybe a late arrival would be nice. But I want to see people! I'm in such a ridiculously good mood! I even actually made conversation with Mom and Dad over dinner and talked to Roxie on the phone for longer than I have in a long time. I am perfectly content.

Friday, January 12, 4:40 p.m.

Overnight, everything froze. And I mean FROZE, not that slick kind of ice that's just packed snow, but crunchy rock-hard sheets that you can skate on. There are footprints frozen into the mud, the ground is mottled and crackles when you walk. School was canceled. Mari came down the trail, and we went to Annie's, then we all walked gingerly into town for lunch. Then after returning to my house, Sam came over, because he had an hour to kill before going to work at the Toy Jungle, so we played Skip-Bo. Basically, it's been a good day.

P.S.

Mari and David broke up!!!! She told me and Annie all about it at lunch. Basically, he got her a koala Build-A-Bear for Christmas (his animal from The Questions) and Mari was so disturbed that he would think she'd be into such a thing that in that one moment she knew they were horribly mismatched.

Plus she said she hung out with Lukas a little bit over winter break and found herself wishing she wasn't attached so she could just "see what happens" with him. I think Annie was secretly excited that M & D had broken up, since everyone knows she's always harbored a secret love for David....

Monday, January 22, 9:47 p.m.

Oh, goodness. I didn't realize it'd been so long since I last wrote. Everything I'm writing right now is terribly dreary.

Hanley announced today that, woe of woes, there is no spring play this year. Instead it'll be the district-wide Community Arts Showcase that happens every few years. Each branch of the art departments at all the schools do a different little event on the same weekend, and it's out in the world, rather than being at school. Hanley had some speech about how it's all about encouraging the wider community to support high school arts. Drama will be performing one-acts, monologues, and scenes at the iDiOM; orchestra and band and choir will have performances at the Mount Baker Theatre; and then Mr. Schmidt has arranged with some local galleries to show student work and have little art opening soirees.

You'd think I'd be excited—because it does sound incredibly exciting and cool, but when Hanley told us about it my heart immediately sank, because she said if you're in more than one arts elective you can only participate in one event.

And since I'm in Drama and Studio Art, I will have to choose between the two. FUCK!

I have been dreadfully sick. It's basically been a reenactment of the plague. I've had this horrible hacking cough that feels like a thousand tiny gnomes are chopping at my throat with ice picks,  and it was so sore I could barely swallow. I went to the doctor and she told me I have strep throat, and on top of that, SCARLET FEVER! Like I'm in *Little House on the Prairie* or something. Anyway, now I'm on antibiotics and feeling better but I have this annoying rash on my neck and chest that hurts and itches and makes my skin really dry, and swallowing is still painful. I'm resting in bed. Well, in Roxie's bed actually. I thought it'd be a little change of scenery from my own. And sometimes I miss her so much now that she lives in Seattle that it's nice to be in her room. Since I'm sick in bed I started reading *White Teeth* by Zadie Smith, which Sam got me, and I think I'm going to read almost the whole thing in a day.

Yesterday, after my fever broke, Sam braved the house of invalids and visited, seeing me **WITHOUT MAKEUP**. Luckily, he seems to like me anyway.

The worst part of contagious disease is the celibacy. I don't know how monks do it. It's so hard not being able to kiss his beautiful face!!!! Why oh why do I date such a germaphobe? Actually, it's probably good that I do because lord knows I'm not one myself.

In other news, my 16th birthday is in two days! And my party is in five! I hope I'm all better by then.

Maybe Sam is biding his time, waiting to talk about anything regarding sex again until my birthday. Then again, maybe not. He's probably not thinking about it at all, and as usual I'm the wild slut with sex on the brain. The other day when I was bored, I was looking at horoscopes online, and my passion one said:

VENUS IS IN AQUARIUS THIS MONTH. YOU AND VIRGO WILL QUENCH ALL OF YOUR SEXUAL THIRSTS AND DESIRES YOU HAVE BEEN HARBORING FOR SO LONG. (!!!)

Um. Sam is a Virgo. I'm an Aquarius.

I love him so much. Is it natural to want to see him every second of the day? I have so much pent-up energy, I want to scream.

Thursday, January 25, 10:26 p.m.

Yesterday was my 16th birthday. Sam bought some condoms from the grocery store. I'm completely in love and at peace. This is all I have to say.

Today was the most wonderful day. Even though my birthday was on Wednesday, today was my party. Roxie came up from Seattle and helped me decorate. We wanted a vintage pink theme.

my Outfit

TIARA

PINK BOLERO

HOT-PINK CHUNKY NECKLACE

my SHINIEST BRACELETS

STRETCHY PINK SHELL BELT

ELEGANT GLOVES

VINTAGE PINK NEGLIGÉE THAT LOOKS LIKE A DRESS

PINK BALLET FLATS

ROXIE MADE PINK FROSTED CUPCAKES IN SILVER PAPERS, WITH SPRINKLES AND TINY PLASTIC PRINCESSES ON TOP FROM ARCHIE MCPHEE IN SEATTLE

TINY TRIANGULAR SANDWICHES (NOT PINK BUT STILL FANCY)

SWEET SIXTEEN party

PINK SPARKLING CIDER (APPLE CRANBERRY) SERVED IN MOM'S FANCY GOLD-RIMMED GLASSES

The whole crew came: Mari, David, Annie, Nora, Jenna, Sam, and even Lukas and Owen and Nathan. Everyone was dressed up fancy, of COURSE! In suits and cocktail dresses, and Annie even wore a glamorous fur coat. Sam looked heartbreakingly handsome in a button-up shirt and slacks, even if his shoes were a little chunky and square-ular.

I know that was kind of telling me I looked beautiful—but I just wish he would say the words. He almost never talks about the way I look, and I know it's superficial of me to want him to at all. Sometimes a silly part of me just wants to know he likes what he sees, and that he doesn't just put up with the way I look because he thinks I'm funny and cool.

We played drama games and bocce ball on the lawn even though it was frigid-cold out (at least it gave me a chance to put on my pink wool 60s jacket). Lukas was so much fun during the drama games—he rarely hangs out with the group since he's usually being all aloof and popular, so it felt like a special treat that he was there. He was so funny and the life of the party. I could tell he kept catching Mari's eye, and it seemed like he was performing FOR her. Annie was all over David, flirting and such, but I could tell David was watching Mari and Lukas too. I wonder if he's not over the whole being-dumped situation.

After everyone left, Sam lingered and I wanted him to stay, and to hang out with him all night, but I could tell Roxie would be pissed if she came up all the way from Seattle and helped me with my party only to be ditched that night, so he went home and she and I went out to Pepper Sisters with Mom and Dad and watched some French movie. When I got in bed Sam had texted me and said, "I hope you had a superlatively spectacular sixteenth." He's so sweet, now I feel bad that I ever complain about him never complimenting my looks. Why must I be so ridiculous and vain!!!!!

Sunday, January 28, 4:34 p.m.

I made the mistake of telling Roxie about Sam and me talking about having sex. I just got off the phone with her. I was shaking and crying and I felt awful. I had wanted to tell her when she was up for my birthday, but I couldn't get up the guts. For the last few weeks, I've been so ridiculously happy, happier than I think I've ever been. It's just felt so good being back at school after winter break with all my friends, and things are so good with Sam and me. I thought maybe she'd see him and get to know him a little bit at my birthday party and decide she wasn't as against us having sex, after all. That she could see he's responsible. But of course she barely interacted with me and my friends at the party. As usual, she helped create the perfect event but then acted like a bitch at it and was totally checked out. I know she's older than us and doesn't think my friends are cool, but I wish at least she could fake it and be nice. She does sometimes but it's in this condescending way that seems so clear to everyone how she ACTUALLY feels.

Everything I was afraid of and knew would happen if I talked to Roxie about sex again has happened.

It's like I opened Pandora's box, and everything I was ever afraid of came flying out and hit me hard. And she threatened blackmail. She said she'd tell Mom unless I promised to wait at least until June. But I couldn't promise. I couldn't say that I wouldn't have sex with him. I was just so angry and upset at the principle of her telling me what to do. Even when I knew the consequences might mean the imminent destruction of my life as I know it. She let me go with plans to "think about it." God, I can't even write. I can't even begin to try to dictate everything going through my head right now. I'm so angry with her and so upset.

Wednesday, January 31, 8:22 p.m.

Today was a horribly tedious day. It was long and uneventful.

Everything is boring and rainy and gray.

I've barely seen Sam at school this week. During drama today we were in different groups the whole class, and at lunch, Annie was being so loud and gregarious that there was no time to connect. So everything I talked about with Roxie on Sunday has just been eating away at me from the inside.

He's been so busy with homework in the evenings that he usually can't talk, and he barely responds to my texts, but I keep sending them any-

way, into what feels like an abyss. I'm so needy. I hate it. I need to try playing hard to get. No more useless texting.

He's going to be out of town this weekend, so if we don't hang out soon, it'll be ages and ages till we can again. I wish his parents would let him go on dates during the week, but they won't let him go out on a school night when there's homework to do.

His parents are so intense. I wish Sam would stand up to them and passionately disagree. But he never does.

FRIDAY, FEBRUARY 2, 11:34 P.M.

I must decide what to do for the Community Arts Showcase. I can't bear to choose between theater and art. All my friends are doing the drama show, of course, and I hate the idea of being left out. Today Mr. Schmidt said, "I really hope you choose the art show." I said I was leaning toward theater, and he looked so sad. And then he got serious, which never happens.

It was kind of intense. And annoyed me because I hate being told what to do. But…I think I feel annoyed because I know he's kind of right. My art fell by the wayside a bit when I got more into drama, but since being in his class I've made so much stuff. And it feels so good. It feels like a part of me is being fed that I didn't know was starving during *Thoreau* and *Tom Jones*, when theater was taking up all my time. And when I think about what I want to do, what I've always envisioned for my life—it's art. Ever since I can remember I've wanted to be an artist. Other people in the drama crew talk about doing theater in college and beyond, but I've only ever wanted a little studio in the woods with high ceilings and wooden floors—days to myself to paint and write and create whatever I want.

After art I had drama class, and I didn't feel like talking to anyone. Everyone was getting excited about the showcase, so I holed up in a dark corner of the theater to think.

I secretly hoped Sam would notice that I was feeling sad. He did. But it took a while. He came over and asked, "Are you okay? You look worried." I said I was fine, because it felt like so much to get into in class. Because it's more than just choosing my allegiance to art or drama of course—it was the conversation with Roxie too, and how little I've seen him all week. I worry that by choosing art for the showcase, I'll lose out on precious time with Sam.

If I'm not in the show with him, won't it just add to my nervousness about his feelings for me?

I think, really, I know that my mind is already made up about what to choose. And that kind of scares me. It scares me that deep down, I know that I would choose my art. Over theater and time with Sam.

Later I was sitting alone in the drama room and he just came up and massaged my shoulders. Just the feeling of his warm hands on me was enough of a connection that I started to feel better about everything. We made REAL plans to hang out tonight after school, not just "I'll call and come over if I can" plans. When he said he could hang out I said, "That makes me happy," and he said, "That makes me happy too."

Sunday, February 4, 2:43 p.m.

Another boring day. Sam is out of town, Nora is doing homework...and no one else can hang out so I'm in my room doing my best to avoid Mom, who is trying to get me to help go through boxes of old books downstairs.

Friday night was good, though. Sam and I walked to my house after school. It's starting to be sunny and springy out, even though it's still cold, and we took a different route than usual, past the university by the creek.

I'M ALMOST ALWAYS IN A GOOD MOOD WITH SAM. I'LL BE STRESSED OUT OR HAVING A BAD DAY BUT THE SLIGHTEST ATTENTION FROM HIM WILL MAKE EVERYTHING BETTER. A LOOK, A WORD. THE TINIEST BIT OF PHYSICAL CONTACT.

When we got to my house, I told him everything about what Roxie had said, about wanting us to wait at least until June to have sex, and threatening blackmail if we don't.

And he just said, "I think we can manage that, don't you?"

And the fact that he was there, holding me and looking into my eyes, telling me that he still liked me and wasn't in the relationship just for sex made me so happy I almost cried. After that it felt like a weight had been lifted off my shoulders, like I had been being pressured, not by Sam, but by me.

I think I've been afraid that if I don't go further with Sam, he will stop liking me.

And then I started thinking about how I really have always had bad self-esteem, and how a year ago I was so much more insecure than I am now, how I could never imagine that someone could like me. And now someone does. And I cried and cried.

I called Roxie after Sam went home and promised we'd wait till June. And as silly as it sounds, everything is back to normal and I'm overwhelmingly happy.

SUNDAY, FEBRUARY 11, 10:15 A.M.

In my room, trying to come up with what I want to do for the Community Arts Showcase this spring.

I chose to go with Studio Art. I was so torn, and so nervous that the crew would feel abandoned by me choosing not to do drama with them. Especially because people like Mari and Lukas are seniors, so it's kind of our last chance to be together in a show. But everyone was very understanding. Especially Sam. Because he is beautiful, wonderful Sam.

But now I have to actually figure out what to make, and so I'm starting to regret my choice—because at least in drama people are in groups and can brainstorm together about what to perform, which sounds nice compared to the utter tedium of sitting alone at my desk racking my brain for any scrap of inspiration. I feel like I'll never have an idea for anything ever again.

There IS a theme to the show, but I feel like that's boxing me in even more. I HATE working within rules for art projects—I want the freedom to make whatever strikes my fancy. Otherwise what's the point of making art??? But instead I have to make "at least five pieces, of any medium or size, exploring the concept of time."

I bet everyone else is just going to draw boring hourglasses and clocks. And I'm annoyed because that's all I can think of too.

Anyway. On Friday Mom drove me over to Sam's house for dinner, and after watching a movie with his family, once it got late and we were alone in the family room, we kissed and kissed. Hard. Almost frantically. As I started to go down on him he whispered, "Wait. Let it last longer," and it was then that I realized that that's what it was all about. Making it last longer. I always get wrapped up in the technicalities, ticking off boxes of what is "supposed" to be happening every time we're together, as if it proves something, that he still likes me because we're doing a, b, and c things....I haven't been just savoring things and making them last. I'm realizing that love, like any other art form, is about learning, and practicing, and paying attention to details. So I tried...to make it last. And it was nice. We kissed slowly and tenderly, and held each other tight. And amazingly, we didn't end up going any further. Just kissed as "Naked as We Came" by Iron & Wine was played from a CD I made him. It was literally like melting. Like we were swirling together into one beautiful whole, just like Joy Penfold said.

"That was the best kiss I've ever had," Sam said. And I said, "I'm glad I have you."

IT WAS THE FIRST TIME HE'D SAID IT.
AND IT MADE ME MORE HAPPY
THAN I CAN EVER DESCRIBE.

LIKE MY HEART GREW
WINGS AND HOVERED ME
OFF THE GROUND.

"I love you, Sam," I said, and I meant it.

WEDNESDAY, FEBRUARY 14, 10:39 P.M.

It's Valentine's Day today—Sam's and my FIRST official one as a couple.

I didn't see him all morning, which made me feel extremely blue. All day people have been getting carnations delivered to them in class. You can pay like $5 for them, and it goes toward funding the prom. I was secretly hoping Sam would get me a carnation even though I usually make fun of people who buy them because they're corny and dyed gaudy, unnatural colors. But he didn't. Which wasn't a surprise but still made me sad.

I saw him at lunch. We ate in the Little Theater with Mari and Nora because it was pouring rain and cold outside, and afterward he asked if I wanted to go on a belated miniversary/Valentine's date tomorrow, which more than made up for not having seen him till then.

I had art class after lunch, and was in such a happy mood. I painted Sam a valentine and listened to music on my iPod.

Sarah Sokolowski, Asher's girlfriend, came in to hang out with her friend Naomi, who's in my class. Naomi is REALLY good at ceramics, so I snooped on what she was making and tried to hear what they were talking about. Sarah had a carnation with her, from Asher, I guess, which surprised me. It was a sickly neon pink. She waved it around, showing

Miró

it Naomi. They both laughed and then she just kind of cast it away, like she didn't even care. I think she was trying to act too cool, but it still seemed kind of ungrateful and mean. Then she and Naomi went outside and smoked Lucky Strikes. Mr. Schmidt doesn't seem to care that much when students fuck around in class or go smoke.

Which usually guilts most people into getting their act together. He's the kind of "cool teacher" who is ACTUALLY cool because he's not trying too hard. He's not afraid to be harsh with people and he has high standards, but he's also really goofy and weird. He likes to joke about all the "creative vases" people make in his classes (i.e., bongs) and he is always excited about what I'm making.

Anyway. In Yearbook, while Asher and I were photo editing, I teased him and said, "I didn't peg you as the carnation type," and told him I saw Sarah with one today. Asher just cracked his knuckles and laughed.

He has this infectious laugh that kind of explodes out in one big "HA!" and it always makes me laugh too. I sometimes wonder if Sarah knows who I am, or if Asher doesn't ever talk about me. After all, I don't ever talk about him to Sam. And it's not like there's any secrets, since we're fully only friends, but sometimes it still feels funny that we have this friendship that's so separate from the rest of our social lives.

WEDNESDAY, MARCH 14, 6:34 P.M.

Last time I wrote was exactly a month ago. I feel a little sad and nostalgic today, but I don't know why because everything has been fine. Every day I feel myself falling deeper in love with Sam, and I could kiss him a thousand times a day and it would never be enough. I can't even remember all the things that have happened in a month. We went on our miniversary/Valentine's date to Pepper Sisters, and sat cozy next to each other on the same side of the booth. It snowed, again. And melted. I went to synagogue with Sam's family last weekend, which was cool but also made me feel silly and not like a real Jew because I didn't know all the prayers and always forget that the books are backward and such.

I also went to Catholic church with Nora and her mom. I'd never been to a church service before. I felt like a heathen fool because I accidentally

ate some bland cracker in the church lobby that was holy or something and not meant for people to take. Nora was mad and embarrassed at first, but then we laughed about it on the way home.

One night a bunch of us went to Nathan Stone's house for a movie night, and for some reason I was so incredibly horny. Lukas had snuck some bottles of his parents' wine, and even just a few sips of it made me feel like I couldn't concentrate on anything anyone was saying. It was like my head was in a fishbowl, and there was this throbbing, pounding heat coming from between my legs. I could tell Sam was horny too, from the way he was making eye contact in a particularly long-lasting way. It was hot and there was this intense tension between us.

IT WAS DEFINITELY THE
BEST HAND JOB I'VE GIVEN SO FAR.

He walked me home, and we hadn't gotten more than a block from Nathan's house before we started making out. It was really starting to feel like spring was on the way. The night air had a flowery, fresh smell, and it was like we were lit up with a wild, spring energy. In an intense and electric rush of adrenaline, Sam pressed me up against one of the neighbors' fences and we kissed. It was late at night and under the stars we pressed our pelvises against each other so hard that I gasped in a kind of nonorgasm orgasm. I jacked him off.

Afterward we felt wild and hyper and ran all the way to my house, giggling hysterically until we reached my front porch, where he kissed me good night.

Even though it's been amazing with Sam, I still worry sometimes. I am an irrational worrier. I need to learn to trust people. I need to trust that Sam's feelings for me will not change at the drop of a hat. He said he loves me and I need to trust him. I need to start having more trust in myself that I'm worthy. Why is it so hard? Does that ever go away?

THURSDAY, MARCH 15, 5:46 P.M.

Do you ever just feel sad for no reason? Like everything is as perfect as can be, then all of a sudden you're just quiet and down? That's how I feel.

I have mood swings, where I go from one extreme to another.

Passion.

Despair.

I thought I would feel less insecure about Sam's feelings for me once he told me he loved me. But I still worry that I'll do something that will make him change his mind. Or that he's just humoring me. Or regrets saying the words. I still get depressed when I don't get enough attention from him, especially at school.

He told me once he thinks school isn't the place for romance. Which I guess is why we don't make out between classes. I know that I shouldn't want to be that couple getting to third base between bells, but a needy, spiteful part of me craves it. It whines that if he's my boyfriend, he shouldn't be able to keep his hands off me, ESPECIALLY if he loves me, right?

I know I should be over wanting that kind of public display now that I know how he feels. But shouldn't HE be the horny one and I should be pushing him away? Not vice versa?

The side of me that I like, the smart and rational me, is able to trust Sam at his word. Trust that he loves me. Know he's happy to be as couple-y as can be outside of school.

But sometimes that voice just gets too drowned out.

Lately I've been convincing myself that other boys like me, so I flirt with them and try to make Sam jealous. It quenches whatever craving I have for that petty flirtation that I don't really get with Sam. He's just so serious. It's not that he's not romantic, he is. Just not in a very playful way. It all comes down to me immaturely trying to vie for his attention. And since he's sensible Sam, he doesn't do a thing about it. Because he shouldn't, really....I just need to be less self-centered and needy, I think. I just need to believe that he loves me, even if he's not all over me during school.

UGH, he is ALL I write about! This is all I think about!!! It dominates my mind and then I don't write about other things that make me happy, like drama and Nora and Mari and the art I've been making....

Although lately most of my art has been about Sam...of inky, starry skies and us floating on clouds. That's what it feels like when we're together—most of the time.

SUNDAY, MARCH 18, 5:50 P.M.

It's been a boring weekend. Sam had to work at the Toy Jungle all day
yesterday, and in the evening, when he could have hung out. I had to go
cover a basketball game for Yearbook with Asher Wilson. Fuck!

I think Mrs. Lynn is starting to catch on that, most of the time, when
she sends Asher and me to cover things, we just kind of fuck off and do
goofy things, so she's started assigning us to sports instead of funner
stuff. I thought I'd be able to hang out with Sam after the game was over,
but then he made plans to go play board games with Lukas and Owen.
I was annoyed, even though I know I shouldn't be, because he almost
never hangs out with his guy friends since he's either always working,
studying, or hanging out with me.

The game was kind of cool, I guess—I'd never been to a basketball
game before. Asher picked me up in his Subaru because it was an
away game in Burlington, so we had to drive almost a half hour to get
there. It was VERY loud, so much shoe-squeaking and ball-bouncing
(ha).

I think Asher purposefully wore the most un-basketball-y outfit possible. We were both kind of the odd ones out at the game.

PURPLE HAT THAT
SAYS "NEW MEXICO
WOMEN OF INFLUENCE"

NEON-GREEN
SWEATER

STRIPED
CONDUCTOR
OVERALLS

SIGNATURE
HIGH-TOPS,
OF COURSE

During intermission, or halftime, or whatever it's called in basketball, Asher said, "Are you hungry?" I said no (lie) because all the food they had at the concession stand looked like what Mom would call "empty calories" and I didn't want him to think I ate junky food even though I was really, really, really hungry. He went and got a bunch of snacks: two corn dogs and nachos with liquid-y, bright yellow cheese, and I wanted them so bad.

I've only ever made nachos at home with melted cheddar, and this was, like, a whole other thing. "I can't believe you've never had the pure magical alchemy that is nacho cheese," Asher said. Then he picked up a cheese-covered chip and held it out. I think, in retrospect, he meant for me to grab it, but for some reason, before I even had time to think about it, I leaned forward and took it from him with my mouth. I could feel one of his fingertips on my tongue for a split second. His eyebrows shot up and I could tell he was surprised.

But he broke the awkwardness by immediately grinning and laughing, which made me laugh too. Then he said, "Now, this is next level," and dipped his corn dog into the melted cheese before rolling it in corn chip bits.

What a goof. I tried it too, though. And it was so good. I shudder to think what Sam, who is a vegetarian, would think about me eating a corn dog, let alone one dipped in liquid cheese. Sam's family is so intense about food it makes Mom look like nothing. At Halloween his little sister isn't allowed to eat any of the candy she trick-or-treats for, and all of them ask for croutons instead of sides of potato chips when they go to the Bagelry for lunch, so that they're not eating something fried, and always order their sandwiches on bialys instead of bagels, because it's "less bread." Is it? At least Mom can eat a bagel and a chip without freaking out.

Asher drove me home after the game and we listened to the new Arcade Fire album, *Neon Bible*, which only came out on the fifth. When "Keep the Car Running" came on, Asher turned up the volume and rolled all the windows down. We both sang along so loud that we were screaming, and I kept laughing because he kept headbanging his wild hair around. It's the kind of song that lights you up and makes your heart race, like anything is possible.

The whole night kind of shook me out of the funk I've been in about Sam not being affectionate enough. There's something so freeing about hanging out with Asher, even though he's mysterious and quiet and weird. I feel like I don't have to be tidy around him like I feel the need to be around Sam. Like I can be loud and wild and Asher doesn't ever roll his eyes like "Oh, Phoebe" the way Sam does sometimes. He just gets on my level instead. And that's why you have friends, I guess, because Sam might not always be able to GET every part of me. And it's okay that sometimes we're each off with our friends and doing our own thing. I need to be more of an independent woman!!!

Monday, March 26, 10:30 p.m.

On Saturday, Jenna and Annie threw a party at Jenna's lake house. I'd never been to one of her parties before, and I wondered whether they get as wild as legends say. I remember last summer when I was dying to go to her parties to be with Owen, and now I get to go with Sam as my date. If only I'd known! I've been worried he wouldn't be able to go because he's been so focused on studying....He keeps flaking on hanging out after school. The other day he said he had a "talk" with his parents where they told him they think weekday afternoons should be for homework only and hanging out with me can happen on Saturdays. What the hell!!!! I know he's a junior so things are more intense than they are for me, but still. I was hoping he'd rebel and be like, "But I told them you're important and I wouldn't do it." But he just said, "I agree."

I don't think he realizes how it makes me feel when he says things like that. Like I'm always coming in second best, me, a real live human BEING, compared to homework.

Anyhoo. He IS coming after all, so I really shouldn't be so negative.

I thought there would be no way in hell Mom and Dad would let me go to Jenna's party. But when I told them I was going with Nora and

Mari, they said, "Okay," I think because they know how ultra conservative (like she doesn't like partying, not like she's a Republican) Nora is, and figured she wouldn't be going anywhere too wild. Plus, Sam is going, and they like Sam and think he's responsible. I also told a billion lies about how parents would be there and everything would be super tame. Nora's mom dropped us off. Luckily, from where she left us on the road, she couldn't hear the loud music that might have made her suspicious.

Jenna lives in a giant, fancy house out by the lake.

The party wasn't even in her real house, but in a little boathouse down on a private dock. Jenna and Annie had turned off all the lights and covered the floor with balloons. The fridge was full of beers, and there was loud music and a strobe light.

I knew immediately that Nora hated it. Because as more people got there, it basically turned into a high school dance but rowdier, without any teachers or chaperones. It wasn't just the drama kids—it was tons of random people from our high school and others I didn't even know. It was packed and sweaty and boiling hot. Everyone wriggled around to rap music. Nora hates things like that. She hates the whole idea of the "kind" of dancing people do. She reminds me of me, last year. You never WANT to go in a dark room with people practically buttfucking and sweating on each other until you WANT to be really close to someone, to feel them, hot and pressed up against you, pelvis to ass.

I wanted to dance with Sam, who showed up shortly after we did, but I felt responsible for Nora. Which I shouldn't have to feel just because we came together. Just because she doesn't have a boyfriend or want to dance "that way" doesn't mean she has to sulk and make me have a shitty time too.... It was one thing after another.

IT'S TOO DARK.

THE STROBE LIGHT HURTS MY EYES.

I HATE THIS MUSIC.

I'M A BAD DANCER.

Finally Sam and I went to dance, and I could feel her eyes boring a hole into the back of my head with annoyance and jealousy. Mari was dancing with Lukas (!), and Jenna and Annie were off with other guys too.

I feel bad but I kind of just started ignoring Nora after a while, because I really didn't want to keep checking on her after every song ended. And it was my first time being at a real high school party, dancing with Sam.

I was scared of the dancing in the beginning, only because I'd never danced like that, but grinding wasn't that bad. And now I'm not afraid to go to school dances anymore.

We danced and danced and got so sweaty. The strobe light made it feel like I was tripping, or like I was in a weird film strip of negatives. All I could feel was the body heat of the people around me, and Sam. His arms tight around my waist, his dick pressing into my back, the beat of

the music pulsing through the two of us like a deep, unifying heartbeat. Everyone knew the words to all the songs and shouted them out, even Sam, who doesn't usually know any lyrics. I guess they know them from going to dances all last year and in middle school. He whispered into my ear, "Do you want to take a break?" and it made me tingle all over.

We escaped into the candlelit bathroom, where up against a wall we kissed and kissed, and our hands went down each other's pants until we came. Well, he did.

Finally I started to feel bad that people might have to pee and so Sam snuck out first, then after a minute I started to too, but before I could open the door it was opened for me by Asher, who was coming in, and we bumped into each other.

I didn't expect him to be at the party because he generally runs with a different crowd. "What are you doing here?" I asked him, but he couldn't hear me because the music was so loud.

He had to say it right in my ear. He was so close I could feel the warmth of his breath and it sent shivers down my spine, which I felt gross about since I'd literally just been making out with Sam in this very spot.

Maybe Roxie is right and now that I've broken the seal on my sexuality, I'm just becoming an untamable slut who gets turned on by anyone being in close proximity to my ear.

"I'm friends with Jenna's brother," he told me. He said that they were technically left "in charge" because her parents weren't home and so were supposed to come down and check on things, "You know, to make sure, like, no one's giving handies in the bathroom and stuff." I could feel that my face went immediately red when he said that. He clearly had known exactly what we'd been doing, even though I thought we had been so sneaky. And as embarrassed as I was (I feel slutty even writing it), part of me almost liked that he'd known. I think because it was the first time he'd ever acknowledged even in a nondirect way that I have a boyfriend and that I'm more than just the sophomore dork he hangs out with in class and talks about music with.

The rest of the night it was like some magic bubble had popped. I went back to Sam and we kept dancing, but the warm blur of music and dancing kept getting interrupted when I'd see Asher out of the corner of my eye, drinking beers or smoking a cigarette out on the dock with Jenna's older brother, Jack. I just kept wondering what he thought of me, and the party, and of Sam. Ugh, I'm being silly and dramatic. WHY do I even CARE! I doubt he even has any thoughts about it at all.

Nora had disappeared, and as it got late I started to feel bad. I looked all around the lake house but couldn't find her anywhere. Finally, I went outside and found her sitting on a plastic chair on the dock and talking to Asher. She was smiling and laughing, but not in the overly dramatic fake way she does sometimes, like she was genuinely enjoying herself all of a sudden. Asher was telling some animated story with a cigarette dangling out of his mouth.

Nora HATES when people smoke. She's always complaining when Annie sneaks behind the Little Theater to have a cigarette, and coughs and waves her hand around dramatically anytime we pass someone smoking on the street, just like my mom does. But here she was not caring a lick that Asher was puffing like a chimney right in front of her face.

Asher ended up giving us a ride home. Nora wanted to go, and I knew I'd be too shitty of a friend if I made her go home alone and stayed to party more with Sam. The devil on my shoulder was trying to convince me to stay, that Nora could take care of herself. But I couldn't leave her. We had planned to sleep over at her house, so if I didn't go home with her now, where would I go?

I awkwardly had to kiss Sam goodbye in front of her and Asher before we left. It was probably in my head, but it was like I could feel Asher's eyes on us, and it made our kiss feel a bit weird and uncomfortable.

Nora sat in front with Asher all the way home since she's taller than me, and he made polite, formal conversation—something he never does when we hang out during Yearbook assignments. I asked Asher if I could pick a CD for the drive home, but Nora said, "I'd actually prefer quiet after all the noise at the party," and Asher said, "Me too."

SINCE WHEN???

Things felt weird with Nora at her house too. I could tell she was annoyed with me, and I felt annoyed with her that she'd wanted to leave early. We usually stay up late talking for hours when we sleep over, and I thought we would have debriefed about everything that happened at the party, but instead she just wanted to go to sleep.

And now I'm on her bedroom floor, under some weird sweaty blanket, listening to her snoring and a clock ticking loudly in the other room. I wonder what Sam is doing and if he's still at the party. I wish I could tell him everything that happened and give him a hug.

What a weird night. I gave a hand job in a bathroom and then got jealous of my friend talking to a guy who I take Yearbook photos with. Does Asher like Nora? Does she like him? I know she thought he was cute before, when we saw him play at the Ben Kweller concert, but that was so long ago and she hasn't talked about him since. He was just so nice and charming to her, where he's usually goofy and cynical with me. I don't know why I'm even bothered. Let them get married for all I care. Sam is who I love, and my heart is aching being away from him now. I hope he's home in bed too and not grinding up against some wayward hussy on the dance floor.

WEDNESDAY, MARCH 28, 4:54 P.M.

Went to Nora's after school today and we played a Nancy Drew computer game (with which we are completely obsessed) all afternoon. I wanted to bring up Jenna's party in a kind of not-bringing-it-up way to test if she was still mad at me for sort of abandoning her while I danced with Sam, so I asked:

I could tell she was kind of excited about it but also feeling shy, and so I tried to play it cool so as not to overwhelm her. We proceeded to hypothesize about whether Sarah is his "real" girlfriend since we only see them together sometimes and I said he never talks about her in Yearbook, and that she's a senior anyway so maybe next year Nora would have a fair shot. I was trying to be really supportive of her crush even though in the back of my head I just kept thinking that there's no way in hell they'd ever work. Asher is like a bad boy in a band, and supposedly some sex-crazed playboy, according to what Annie said. I mean, *I* don't think he is, but judging by the way girls were looking at him at the BK concert, many seem to think he's a sex god. He smokes cigarettes for god's sake!!! Even I think that's gross, let alone someone like Nora. Well, he occasionally smokes them....I don't think he's, like, addicted. Nora is just...so pure. She's the untouched mountain lake. And Asher... Asher is like rapids leading to a waterfall. It's hard to picture them ever working, even if Sarah was out of the picture. But I'm being too much of a grouch. I must be supportive, even if it does mean Nora's heart might be broken.

THURSDAY, MARCH 29, 2:15 P.M.

It's beautiful out. All sunny and springlike. I'm lying out in the back-yard. Sam is supposed to call, and he might come over. But he seemed more inclined to go home and read his history textbook.

He just called.

He's not coming.

He's going home to sleep.

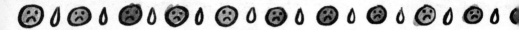

Friday, March 30, 11:03 a.m.

All I do these days is cry. I feel like I'm always on the verge of tears. I even cried a few minutes ago at school telling Nora about being sad that Sam can never hang out.

2:39 p.m.

Sam said in class that he might come over later. But I know he won't. He'll realize he has too much homework, I'm sure. He has to know that I'm upset by now. Every day this week he's said he'd try to come over after school, and every day he hasn't. Maybe he has just stopped liking me. Nora said I should talk to him about it. And I fully intend to, once we're actually alone together. I just feel like we'll never be alone together again. He's going to Portland this weekend with his family to see his uncle, so we won't have any time to talk. I want it all to go away and go back to the way it used to be.

SATURDAY, MARCH 31, 4:57 P.M.

Just as I thought, Sam had to study yesterday after school again and couldn't hang out. It was our last chance to see each other before he left for Portland today to visit his uncle. I know he's not going to be gone long, and that we'll be able to text and talk, but it's not the same. There's so much that I want to say in person. That I'm scared to say.

Dear Sam,

I don't know why I'm writing this letter to you since I doubt I'll ever send it. It's about a fear I have sometimes. Or sadness. Or a ridiculous feeling of neglect brought on by an overly active self-pity complex and irrationally worrisome mind.

During the school week when we don't hang out often it builds, then every Friday I mean to talk to you about it, but then after school we hang out and your during-the-week cold shoulder is gone, so I put it out of my head until the next week. It's kind of a cycle. But this weekend I'm not seeing you at all, and so it's just building and building and getting worse.

Here is what I feel: that sometimes you don't like me very much, or that you avoid spending time with me. There have been days when you have said nothing to me at all, or some days when I look at you and you seem to be annoyed by the things I do. I know that you don't think school is the place for romance, and neither do I, but it's the only place we see each other sometimes. And I personally don't think it's wildly inappropriate to acknowledge my existence from time to time. I'm exaggerating, I know. You acknowledge me. We even talk and have lunch together with friends. And I know that you are busy with homework and have a job. And I know you think good relationships need space, which I do too. But every day I look around at all the boys who can't keep their hands off their girlfriends, and I don't know if maybe I'm doing something wrong and that's why you take your hand away when I try to hold it when we're at school.

Maybe I'm not supposed to think about you all the time or wonder what you're doing. You probably don't think about any of this, and I know you're not trying to hurt me. I'm sorry. I wish I knew how to be normal. Only four times you've initiated saying "I love you." I'm a freak that I'm even keeping track. I'm secretly afraid that if I tell you these things, you'll break up with me. That you'll leave me for someone cooler, who doesn't care about this stuff as much. Sometimes I feel so inferior around you, or like a chore.

But now you just texted me, "Goodnight, I love you." Which makes me feel ridiculous for writing all this shit. Why can't I just trust you. I love you too, I do, I do, I do. I must stop my emotional nonsense.

♥ love, P ♥♥

Tuesday, April 3, 3:44 p.m.

I feel so much better than I did last time I wrote. I was feeling so depressed.

Last night I finally had a creative breakthrough with my Community Arts Showcase project—and just in time, because Mr. Schmidt wants to approve what we're going to do by Friday so that we can get started on our collections over spring break!

I've been so frustrated about having to conform to a specific theme and write a whole proposal and artist statement and stuff. Even though it's good practice for the "real" art world, I guess. I just kept getting trapped in my own head. No idea has felt good enough. I've been getting so jealous of everyone in drama, who are already blocking out scenes and having so much fun in their groups.

I told Mr. Schmidt that I couldn't think of anything, and he just said, "There are some problems that can only be solved once you start to draw," which annoyed me because how am I supposed to just start drawing if I don't have an IDEA first???

Anyway. After dinner yesterday I went up to my room and listened to Sufjan and lay on my bed doodling random people in my sketchbook. Dad and I used to play this game while waiting for a table at a restaurant where one of us would draw a person and then pass the drawing to the other person, who would write their name and either a little bio or story about them. And I was kind of doing that, drawing a face then coming up with little firsthand stories about magical moments in their lives—*Our Town*-esque moments, if you will.

And then I realized—why couldn't this be my project? *Our Town* moments make you feel like time is standing still...but, at the same time, make you so aware of the ephemeralness of the split second you're in. So if each portrait and story captures that feeling, wouldn't they fit into the theme of "time"?

And then it was like a dam had broken and I couldn't stop. I sketched out rough drawings of all the people I wanted to include and got lost in who each of them was. The writing was kind of like poetry, I guess—although I've never written poetry before. But it FELT like what I imagine writing poetry would feel like....I was just kind of caught up in the flow and rhythm and feeling of the words.

All in all I made ten sketches. I am really excited about them, but I also feel slightly embarrassed to show them to Mr. Schmidt. Because they feel so intimate, I guess. But maybe that's a good sign.

Monday, April 9, 11:36 p.m.

It's officially spring break! Today, Sam came over, and it was such a treat to hang out early in the day since there wasn't any school. And nice too because we had so much time before Mom and Dad would be home from work. We curled up naked in bed and napped. He was so warm—I wish we could've stayed there forever. I honestly do love him so much. Next month we will have been together half a year. That seems like such a long time. I am blissful. ♡

Friday, April 13, 1:20 a.m.

I don't really know where to begin—what, with all of this spring break nonsense! So far I've been to TWO Passover Seders, camped out in the rain, and just enjoyed lazing about doing nothing at all.

The first Seder I threw at Mari's house. Or, I should say, I co-threw it with Mari. Mari's family are very relaxed Jews, like us (Sam's term "semi-Semites" has caught on in our families), and so the only holidays we really do are Hanukkah and Passover, with maybe some apples and honey thrown in for Rosh Hashanah. The whole drama crew came, most of whom hadn't been to a Seder before, so Mari and Sam and I had to explain that it's where we tell the story of the Jews' exodus from Egypt, and that it would be about 23949084 years until we ate because we had to read through the whole Haggadah first and just eat ceremonial bits of matzo and charoset and bitter herbs before finally getting to the good stuff (roasted lamb and potato kugel that Mari's mom helped us cook).

SEDER PLATE

LAMB SHANK BONE
(BUT OURS IS A FAKE DINOSAUR BONE FROM THE VANCOUVER SCIENCE MUSEUM GIFT SHOP.)

EGG →

ORANGE →

→ MAROR
(HORSERADISH. EW. I SKIP IT.)

CHAROSET
(APPLES, NUTS, WINE)

KARPAS
(PARSLEY)

BITTER GREENS

MARI'S PARENTS LET US HAVE WINE (EVEN NORA HAD SOME!) AND SO EVERYONE WAS PRETTY ROWDY BY THE END OF THE SEDER.
DAY-DAY-ENU, DA
PEACE
HAGGADAH
HAGGADAH

I wish I could say it would have been as
much fun if Mom and Dad were there,
but it wouldn't because we DEFINITELY
wouldn't have been able to drink wine. I don't
really like wine. Especially red wine. And would
really rather have Kedem grape juice, which is what
Mom always gets. But I drank it anyway because it's fun
to feel buzzed. We also had a rambunctious hunt all over the house for the
hidden afikomen, and finally found it inside a Paul McCartney record
cover in the living room. After the Seder and dinner we all collapsed in
the living room and talked and hung out till people were sober enough
to drive or walk home. (Mari's parents were very strict about that, you'll
be glad to know.)

The next night was the campout, which was so fun. It's finally starting
to be warm enough to be outside—all the apple trees are blooming. The
whole crew pitched tents in Nora's yard and roasted hot dogs over a fire
for dinner.

Nora's house and property are so cool—her family has lived on it for generations, and so there's all kinds of amazing old stuff lying around: vintage tractors, a super-old fire engine, and of course her giant swing, which her grandpa installed high in the trees with his logging spikes. When it got dark we played Sardines all over the property and in the woods, and it was so fun and we kept psyching each other out getting giddy and scared because it was so creepy being in the woods at night. There was lots of hysterical laughter and screaming and it was très fun.

I was hoping I'd get to be in the same tent as Sam, but of course Nora shut me down because she thought it would be too scandalous. After we'd all finally gone to sleep, it ended up POURING rain, and we all had to run inside, screaming and carrying our bedding through the rain. We ended up making nests on the couches and floor in the living room.

The second Seder I went to was with Sam's family. I'm actually starting to think they like me. Like, last night his mom asked my opinion on how she should wear her scarf, AND on what movie to watch. It's not like I ever thought they necessarily hated me, but they have this slightly cold, intellectual vibe that can be hard to read. I guess I'm just getting to know them better as time goes on....

Sam. Sam. Sam. Sam. I miss him, even though I was with him most of the day.

Anyway.

The Seder was good—but super weird. Mostly because it turned out that Asher Wilson was there. It was Sam's parents' friend's house, and there were a bunch of different families there. Sam and I were sitting with a few other people at what was turning into the kids' table when Asher and his family came in. I'd never seen them before—only imagined what they were like from Annie's description of them being rich and very relaxed about sex. His mom just looked like a classic Bellingham hippie mom, with long, wild hair like Asher's and a gap in her front teeth. His dad was just regular-looking with glasses.

Asher came and sat with us and said "Hey" like he was totally unsurprised to see me. And I said, "Hi." Then he casually said "Hey" again to Sam. I didn't even know that they knew each other at all. I mean, I know they're in the same grade—but neither of them has ever mentioned the other in any significant way. "I didn't know you're Jewish," I said to Asher, and he just smiled and said, "Shalom, comrade."

Apparently, Asher's and Sam's parents go way back, so they've known each other peripherally their whole lives. Asher being there made the whole night feel really strange, like I couldn't quite be who I normally am around Sam because I also felt like I had to be the ME that I am around Asher, and I didn't know how to balance the two. Asher kept cracking me up singing the prayers in ways that different musicians would and making me guess who he was.

I felt like I shouldn't laugh as much as I wanted to because I could tell that Sam didn't know any of the singers we were talking about, and I didn't want to make him feel left out.

Sam doesn't really listen to music, which I need to change.

All he has on his iPod is *The Matrix* soundtrack. I don't understand how he can just not be into it??!! He's always saying he just doesn't really have time to listen.

PLAYLIST of the moment:

- *A Better Son/Daughter, Rilo Kiley*

- *Wake Up, Arcade Fire*

- *Sons and Daughters, The Decemberists*

- *Concerning the UFO Sighting near Highland, Illinois, Sufjan Stevens*

- *Eyes, Rogue Wave*

- *I Don't Love Anyone, Belle and Sebastian*

- *King of Carrot Flowers Pt. 1, Neutral Milk Hotel*

- *Wasted and Ready, Ben Kweller*

- *I Was Born (A Unicorn), The Unicorns*

Sunday, April 15, 10:10 p.m.

Today was the last day of break.

I smoked yesterday. Weed. For the first time.

The day started with Sam coming over. It was all planned out that we were going to go to Annie's to smoke, but we had a couple of hours to kill so first we cuddled in my bed. Outside it was pouring rain and it was so nice lying together and listening to the rain on the roof. I'm going to say we made love. Even though that usually means sex, which we didn't have, depending on what you consider "sex" to be. We made love. Afterward we sat naked and were quiet. There was no embarrassment. It was beautiful, like we disappeared into a different world. We did have to tear ourselves out of it, though, when we heard the sound of Mom's car crunching gravel in the driveway. We got dressed as fast as we could and ran down the stairs so that we'd just casually be hanging out on the couch by the time she got inside.

Then Nora and Mari came over and we all played Balderdash. It was super nice to be inside with friends on a wet day—it felt like last fall when we'd all get cozy inside and drink tea and play games. Afterward Nora left, and Sam and Mari and I had dinner with Mom and Dad, and then

331

walked in the rain to Annie's house, and I talked about how we felt kind of guilty because we were going to Annie's to smoke. And Nora didn't know. We specifically didn't tell her about the plans because we knew she wouldn't have approved.

Annie was smoking a cigarette on her front porch when we got there.

Sam was upset, and so was I, because we all have been trying to get Annie to quit smoking cigarettes since they're so bad for you. She always says she has but then sneaks them now and then. We all went inside, where David already was, and proceeded to spend the next TWO HOURS calling every minorly stonerish person we could think of trying to find weed.

Finally Annie talked to someone who said that a kid named Nick might know, and so she called Nick and after a while he showed up on the porch with a "dime bag" and we completed the exchange. I felt really hyper and jittery the whole time, because it felt so weird to be in on a *DRUG DEAL*, but also excited.

It was Sam's first time (which surprised me) and mine, but everyone else was a seasoned pro. We smoked it huddled on her back porch so we could stay out of the rain.

The smoke felt like it was shredding my throat to smithereens, and I coughed for about 700 years, but I kind of liked it, and it got better with my next hit. Then when we were done Annie said, "CASHED!" and bit into the apple.

"Eat the evidence!" David said, and we all laughed and took bites till it was gone.

All I remember about being stoned was how beautiful everything was, like I was seeing it all through weird, warped goggles that added a dreamy haze to the world around me.

EVERYONE'S EYES LOOKED SO NICE AND SPARKLY, AND THE SNACKS WE ATE TASTED AMAZING, BETTER THAN ANYTHING I'D EVER HAD BEFORE.

Time felt weird too. We were in the kitchen eating for what felt like hours but also it could have been only a minute or so. Then we all went upstairs and collapsed into a heap in Annie's bed and laughed so hard at I don't even know what. It was so much fun. It was fun seeing Sam get so loopy. He can be goofy sometimes, but especially lately, with school ramping up toward the end of the year, he's been in a more serious mode, and it seemed like he was really truly relaxed. After it wore off people started to go home. Sam had to leave right from Annie's, so Mari and I walked home together, our arms linked, laughing.

I'm so sad that she's graduating and won't be at school next year. It has felt so good being friends again, and like we're really just hitting our stride and now she'll be gone. Annie too. I know I'll have Jenna and Nora still, and maybe there will be new friends who start drama as well, but it won't be the same. It won't ever be quite the same.

When I got home, even though I wasn't stoned anymore, I felt an overwhelming itch to paint. And so even though it was late, I started working on my collection for the Arts Showcase. I took little bits of paper and fabric I'd been saving because I liked the patterns, and glued them right onto my canvas, like the piece I made a while back with the shredded paper bits. I worked off the sketches I'd made for my project proposal, decorating the portraits with flowers and collaged shapes, and then with a Sharpie wrote the poems and stories, filling every bit of the negative space. I couldn't stop—I worked until at least 3 a.m. It was like I was under an enchantment, and I just HAD to work until whatever trance I was in lifted. I feel most like myself in those moments. Most like the me I was when I was a kid, the dorky homeschooler drawing all day long. Most like the me that I want to be when I'm grown up. Most like the parts of myself that I'm proudest of now. I stop worrying, stop thinking...about Sam, and school, and friends, and Mom and Dad and Roxie, and I just kind of...go. I don't know how else to explain it.

SATURDAY, APRIL 21, 10:51 A.M.

When I haven't written in a long time I think I'll have so much to say, so I sit down to write and forget everything that has happened to me. It's been a week since I last wrote—but I don't even know what all I've done.

Yesterday Sam came over and we lay in bed for over two hours. It was pouring rain but we were so warm. I wonder if years from now I'll be able to remember how soft his cheeks and neck were, how they smelled, how it felt to kiss him.

Do you ever think about all the things you'll miss when you're old?

Like kisses and the spicy scent of witch hazel blossoms or the smell of babies' hair...the brisk, salty sea air that rolls off the bay and the sound of rain pattering on leaves...

And I wonder if I'll ever get to be old, or if maybe the sea level will rise over Bellingham and the sun will burn the po-

lar bears and humans up and we'll go extinct. Or just kill each other off. Maybe it is the lucky ones who get to grow old and stew in nostalgia.

When I am an old woman, I will wear a braid over the top of my head, and I will be surrounded by daffodils. And I will remember Sam, and his soft, salty skin. And his dark hair glowing in the sun. I am so afraid of forgetting.

"Kiss me," I will say to him tomorrow. "Why?" he'll ask, caught off guard. I will smile. "What if you never get to see me again?"

Sunday, April 29, 7:15 p.m.

I am sick. Today was Dad's Woodstock Farm Conservancy thing. I wasn't sick this morning, or when I got to the event, and I was able to sit through Dad giving his talk about preservation of green spaces and history and blah blah, but then afterward, when everyone was milling around talking, I started feeling like I was going to barf.

All of Dad's work people were there and a bunch of our family friends too. Even Sam came.

My limbs felt heavy and collapsible, and Sam said "Oh dear" when he heard my teeth chattering, and he put his arms around me. After Dad's talk was over I lay down on the grass outside and he put his coat over me and said, "It's gonna be okay." But I just kept feeling worse.

THEN I THREW UP IN FRONT OF SAM!!! 😫

He rubbed my back and then went to get Mom, and some water. That was about 3:30 or something and I've been in bed ever since. Having hot flashes and chills. Roxie was up from Seattle to visit her boyfriend, who is leaving soon for Alaska because he's a commercial fisherman. They came in and read me *Madeline*. Now I'm feeling a lot better because I had some Tylenol. I called Sam, just to hear him talk. I shut my eyes and he told me all the things going on at his house, until I had a picture in my mind. He was having his computer read him the review for the AP US History test, which he likes to freak out about lately. I can feel my pulse throbbing through my whole body.

Tuesday, May 1, 8:45 p.m.

I am all better, but now Sam is sick. That's what comes from saliva swapping when you're still not quite recovered, I guess. I hate the term "saliva swapping." I can't believe I wrote it.

I smoked again today. With Annie. It was a spliff. Half tobacco, and just enough weed to get you high. I walked over to her house after school and we hung out for a while in her room, talking. Annie has really grown on me. I used to think of her mostly as a loud, annoying gossip, but she can be really sweet and funny and fun, especially when you're hanging out with her one-on-one or in small groups, and especially without boys. (She's like a whole different person around boys.)

Annie had the weed squirreled away. It was kind of old and dry, she said, but it's not like I'd know the difference. She rolled it with the tobacco and we took it out to her backyard, where there's a little bamboo/tree thicket next to the fence. We stood in there and since I'd never done a joint before, she showed me how to light it while sucking in. I think I felt high, a little—it was definitely very mild. Not as strong as the last time. I felt just a little buzzy and spaced out around the edges, and everything Annie said made me laugh. It didn't last long, though. By the time I walked home the feeling was mostly gone, and after it had completely worn off I called Sam to tell him, and that's when he told me he is sick. His AP testing starts soon and he's so worked up about it. I can't WAIT for tests to be OVER. I'm so tired of hearing about it. Sunday after next is our six-month anniversary; we are going out for a fancy dinner somewhere that Saturday. I wanted to go out to a movie too, except Mom's annoying choir concert is that night, which greatly restricts everything, and I have to go because I missed her last concert. I signed up for driver's ed. I'm excited to learn to drive even though Roxie already secretly taught me a little bit in the Value Village parking lot. It's been almost a year since I started this journal. I can't believe how much of the book I've already filled! I hate to look back on those entries about Owen and David, though—I can't believe I liked David.

P.S.

I saw that lady Olivia Wormwood from the iDiOM play again!!!!!

I was downtown with Mari doing homework and drinking tea at Fantasia yesterday, and she came in and hung out with the barista for a long time, talking like they were friends. She has cool tattoos on her arms that I couldn't see before and was wearing an amazing out-fit again. I must admit I've looked at her Myspace a few more times since the last time I wrote about her. I'm a stalker, I know!!!!!! She has changed her profile song to "Maps" by the Yeah Yeah Yeahs, but that's it.

STALKER ALERT.

Tuesday, May 8, 10:55 p.m.

I'm stressed out. I'm sorry it's been a week since I last wrote. Sunday is Sam's and my six-month anniversary, and I'm still worried he'll be too busy studying for his AP tests to go out the night before. I haven't really seen him all week, and I'm telling myself to be patient because tomorrow is his first test, and after that he'll have less on his plate. I know I'm freaking out for no reason, I just need to focus on my own work and go to sleep.

The work I'm supposed to be doing is for the Community Arts Showcase, which is at the end of the month. We have to turn in all our work by the 24th!

In class yesterday Mr. Schmidt told us where our shows would be, and my group is at a cool gallery downtown. I am so nervous that my art won't be sophisticated enough to show there and keep procrastinating making my last two paintings because I just know they won't be as good as I want them to be.

I'm just so tired of everything I make. I wish I could just rip every painting to shreds and start over again.

I was so obsessed with the way they were turning out at first. It felt like such a big breakthrough, but now I just can't stand any of it.

But of course now there's no time and I know that the only option is to just keep going and finish the paintings up. Even if I feel like I can't bear it.

I'm going to sleep now.

Sunday, May 13, 12:30 a.m.

Today is Sam's and my six-month anniversary. And tonight (well... last night, it's after midnight now) he was relaxed enough to go out!!!! AND...he asked me to

JUNIOR PROM!

Ever since prom season "started" I've been wondering if he was going to ask me, but he's been so busy that I also felt like it wasn't on his mind. Jenna asked Tim, who is in our drama class this semester (I think they'll start dating soon...they've been majorly flirtatious), and Annie was asked by Nathan (!!!). If Sam wasn't a junior, I wouldn't be getting to go at all. I can't believe my first real school dance is going to be a PROM!

The way he asked me was so romantic. The guys often make a big deal out of it, like getting a girl flowers or surprising them in class. It all started this morning.

I went down only to find a letter in a tiny envelope telling me to walk down to the candy store to collect my next clue.

Good morning, Phoebe, oh so kind. The candy store is where you'll find, a little something just like you; sweet and nutty... and oh yeah... a clue!

I got dressed as fast as I could and ran down the hill. It was a scavenger hunt! At the candy store I told them I was there for a clue, and they got all excited and handed me another tiny envelope, along with my favorite kind of fudge (vanilla walnut). I ran around to three more businesses collecting little items and clues, the last of which said this:

A forest of playthings is where to head now. There assemble a puzzle and flip it some how...

THE TOY JUNGLE!!! Once there I had to assemble a little wooden puzzle, flip it over, and then on the back it read, PROM? And then Sam came out with a bouquet of flowers and all his coworkers clapped!!!

I said yes. And gave him a kiss. I'm so excited.

I need to find a dress!!!!!

Then tonight we had our anniversary dinner, and it was the best date we've ever been on. We talked and laughed and I was so happy just to spend time together after a week of him being in his AP test daze. I can't believe he found time for such an elaborate prom ask while he's been so busy! After dinner we got gelato and took the bus over to Mom's choir concert, which we had decided would just become part of our date. It was a wonderful night.

Monday, May 14, 6:22 p.m.

I'm gonna have to go to dinner any minute—but I had to write because I forgot to tell you that I figured out what I'm going to do about a dress for prom! Grandma is helping me MAKE one. I just feel like none of the ones in stores are my style. I went with Annie and Jenna to the mall last night and they tried things on. There wasn't much in my size, especially that I liked, and most of the dresses just looked trashy and not what I want. I want a vintage-y tulle, old-movie-star-type dress. But every time I see them in thrift stores they're like a size -000, made for some old-timey stick.

I told Grandma what I was thinking of because she can sew, and she said she'd help, and so today I sketched out some ideas.

After school Sam and Mari and Nora came over and we played games. It was warm enough to sit outside at the picnic table! One of Sam's jobs at the Toy Jungle is to test the new games they get in so the staff can make recommendations and review them, so we played a bunch of weird random games that he was really intense about explaining the rules of, like he was teaching a class. It was fun, though.

SAM KEPT GETTING (PLAYFULLY) ANNOYED AT ME BECAUSE I KEPT CALLING THESE LITTLE GUYS "PEOPLE" WHEN THEY'RE REALLY CALLED *MEEPLE*.

Saturday, May 19, 10:15 p.m.

I got my driver's permit!! I've driven twice since, to REI and downtown, both times with Dad. ALSO...

Thespian Society initiation is super secretive, and I knew it was the time of year that it usually happens, but everyone who's already initiated had been mum's-the-word on when it would be. I knew I have enough drama credits now to officially join, though, so I was expecting it at some point. Then last week I got a mysterious call from Lukas.

356

It was both funny and sent shivers down my spine. Then they handed me an unlit candle and we waited for the rest of the initiates to come (Jenna, Tim, and Freya). Then we went to the drama room, which was dark except for tons of candles and Christmas lights and scarves masking all the whiteboards and posters and stuff. In the center of the room on a podium was a big bowl filled with sand, with a big candle in the middle.

After Lukas said a few things, each person stood and read little passages about drama and what being a Thespian means. After speaking, they lit a candle and stuck it in the bowl of sand. Then our "initiator" stood up—Mari was mine.

"I think we can all agree that the Little Theater has gotten a little brighter since Phoebe started doing plays," she said, and I already felt like I was going to cry. She went on about how I'm funny, and so creative, and such a loyal friend. Everyone around her was smiling and looking right at me with these bright, shining looks. Especially Sam. And it made my heart hurt. I don't know how I'm going to do next year without Mari and all the other seniors.

When she was done, I tried to subtly wipe away my tears, then lit my candle, and we all signed our names on the school Thespian roster.

Then we went out to the theater, and all our parents were there with food and drinks and everyone cheered. It was so nice. We all hung out at Mari's after and Sam walked me home. We made out intensely on the trail, kissing and holding each other so tight. Then our hands went into each other's pants. When we were done, he kissed my forehead and we kept holding each other. I burrowed into his neck, took in his warmth and smell. Just me and Sam. I love him and he loves me. I will write about the rest of the weekend tomorrow.

There's a lot to say. Good night!

WEDNESDAY, MAY 23, 9:25 A.M.

I just DROVE to school with Mom, in her NICE car, not the van, which I've been driving with Dad. Though I definitely prefer driving with Dad. Mom is a lot more uptight.

I'll write what I can now about the rest of last weekend, but I'll probably have to continue later.

On Saturday, I got to be IN the spring parade downtown! The school did a float that went behind the band. It was mostly cheerleaders and star athletes on it, but the Thespians got to dress up in outfits from the costume closet to represent the drama department (we went with cowboys and "Old West"–type ladies in bonnets, because that's what there was the most of from a production of *Oklahoma!* years ago).

It was so much fun! Then afterward we all went to Win's Drive-In for burgers and shakes, still in our cowboy gear.

Annie had driven Sam and me there, and after we left we kept hanging

out, just driving around feeling the warm spring air and listening to music and having such a good time. We were sort of trying to find a party to go to, but even Annie, the master partier, couldn't find any after making a bunch of calls, so we mostly were just joyriding. I told Mom and Dad that we were watching a movie at Annie's house, because I knew they wouldn't like it if I said we were just kind of driving around aimlessly. It was getting close to my curfew, though, and we were having such a good time that I called and asked for an extension.

...I lied, obviously. But they love it when I plan ahead, so naturally, they ate it up. What could possibly go wrong?

Thursday, May 24, 9:40 a.m.

Sorry I haven't continued until now. Anyway. Shit. The bell just rang and I have to go to class so I won't be able to write until after school again.

4:18 p.m.

I'm tired of having to keep coming back to Saturday night. Long and short of it: we got in a CAR CRASH.

It was around 12:30 and we were taking Sam home. He lives across town and Annie lives near me, so it was also just kind of an extension of our drive-around. We were out on Lakeway Drive and Annie had her blinker on, about to turn left. But then she decided not to turn, because we were mixed up about where we were, so she decided to turn right instead, but there was already someone passing us on the right, and we hit them.

It wasn't super high speed or anything, and the cars didn't really get messed up. But it was still so scary. We both pulled over on the side of the road and the guy who we'd hit was super weird and out of it. He kept just kind of muttering about how he didn't want to get the cops involved and that he was so sorry, even though it was fully Annie's fault because he'd been legally passing.

Since we hadn't really messed up his car Annie gave him her number, but the guy said it was all okay, and we went our separate ways. He had seemed like he really didn't want any attention called to himself, by calling the police or even getting insurance involved. It was super sketchy and when we got back into the car we all felt jittery and hysterical and so tense. It was like this fun spell we'd been under driving around town and singing with the windows down had been completely broken. We drove Sam home in silence and it wasn't until he got out that I realized I'd been death-grip-clutching his hand. Annie was trying to defuse the tension by laughing it off, saying things like "WELLLLLL, that was wild! I can't believe that guy hit us!" even though it was definitely her fault. We barely talked all the way back to my house after we dropped off Sam. I was just so shaken. I wasn't really mad at her—I know it was just a mistake. But it made me not want to just drive around with friends at night anymore. This is what I get for lying to Mom and Dad. I knew they'd hate what we were doing and this is exactly why!

Anyway. We were nervous a day or so after it happened and worried that Annie's parents would notice scratches on the car or the guy would call her and want money or something, but luckily nothing has happened. I'm so glad it wasn't any worse.

FRIDAY, MAY 25, 8:19 P.M.

It's starting to be that time of year, when things are wrapping up at school and it's all just a busy blur! The Community Arts Showcase is **TOMORROW!!!** I am so excited but also sad, because my show is at the same time as the one-act show that the drama department is doing. They'll be able to come to my show after theirs ends, but I have to be at the gallery all evening with my group.

I dropped all my work off with Mr. Schmidt in class yesterday. The next time I see it, it will be on gallery walls…! It's strange knowing that the public will be looking at things I made, and even buying them if they want. The paintings feel so CLOSE to me in a way, like they're a part of my body. It kind of makes me want to die knowing people will be looking at them and reading the poems. Part of me wants to just hide them away. But I'm also excited for them to be out in the world.

Today I went to Grandma's after school and we worked more on my dress for junior prom! After looking through a bunch of old patterns to try to find something like what I want, we ended up just going rogue and making it up. And it's turning out PERFECT.

I'm going to make a little felt flower boutonniere for Sam too. I think everything will be ready in time—prom is so soon! Nora said her mom has some vintage red high heels I can borrow, and I got red lipstick from the Aveda salon.

I think Nora feels a little left out that we're all going to prom and she doesn't have a date. I wish someone would have asked her. I kept telling her she should just come on her own, but she said, "No, that would be so awkward. I don't like dances anyway," which is true. And a part of me was relieved because I knew if she came she'd have a terrible time and it would make me feel like I couldn't relax.

I'm so excited!!!!! Sam has already rented his tux. I can't wait to see how he looks.

I CAN'T WAIT FOR PROM!!

Sunday, May 27, 11:34 a.m.

The Community Arts Showcase was last night!

I was feeling so down about it being the same night as the drama show, but all of that kind of faded away once I got to the gallery.

My doubts about my work sort of faded too. Like, I could see the things I wish I'd done differently, but mostly seeing it hung up all professionally in the fancy space just made me feel kind of giddy and proud. Although knowing everyone else was seeing it too made me want to be invisible a little bit.

It was one of the first really summery nights of the year, so there were tons of people out and about, and I felt so jittery and nervous because it felt so much more REAL being at an actual gallery than at the school! They were even serving grapes and cheese and sparkling cider in hard plastic cups.

There are three other people from Studio Art in my group: Asher's girlfriend's friend Naomi, someone else who does ceramics, and a guy who only makes stoner-y paintings of frogs. I'd made the most work by far, and I couldn't help but wish it was my own solo show, rather than

being lumped in with other people whose work was so different than mine.

My whole family came—Mom and Dad with flowers, Roxie and her boyfriend, even Grandma stopped by. Mari's and Sam's families came on their way to the one-act show, and I was embarrassed because Sam's dad kept saying, "Looks familiar" about a painting of someone who looked like Sam. It was such a whirlwind of talking and smiling and mingling with students and teachers and family and people who were walking around downtown. Sarah Sokolowski came, on her own, to hang out with Naomi for a while.

And the best part is that I SOLD three paintings! Sam's parents bought the one that looked like Sam, and Mr. Schmidt bought another. "I gotta get one now while I can still afford your work," he said, and winked. And then a complete stranger bought one too! It made me want to cry.

Toward the end of the night, Asher Wilson came, in a group of cool older hipsters I've seen around town—including OLIVIA WORMWOOD. I nearly DIED! I wonder if they know each other from the music scene?? She spent a long time looking at my work and pointing things out to her friends. My heart was beating so fast I thought it was going to explode. I was so focused on watching her that I barely noticed Asher come up to me, until he said, "Hey" and made me jump.

Even though we're friends, it still feels like sometimes there's some giant balloon of awkwardness between us that could pop at any time. Like there's so much that's unsaid, but I don't even know what.

I wondered why he and Sarah came separately. We fell into an awkward silence, and while we were just kind of standing there, there was a big commotion as the whole drama crew rolled in. Their show must have ended, and they still had bits of stage makeup on. They kind of enveloped me, and Asher drifted away, but it had been so awkward that I didn't mind. It was so good to see them all. But I also felt a weird self-consciousnesses about what Olivia and Asher and their cool friends thought of everyone's rowdiness and unhip style.

As she was leaving, Olivia TALKED TO ME!!!

And Asher, who was behind her, gave me a kind of proud look.

All in all, it was a great night. Sam gave me a ride home from the show, and we made out in my driveway and it was so nice. I wish he could have come in, but Mom and Dad were already asleep, so I knew it was too late.

THURSDAY, MAY 31, 9:49 P.M.

I'm writing with a head-
lamp on as if the power has
gone out, but it hasn't. It
just feels good to be in the
dark.

A huge thunderstorm is
going on. It's been weirdly
warm and humid for at least
a week, and it feels like the
weather reached a breaking

point and just exploded into this storm. It was just raining harder than
it's ever rained in my memory.

I just had a huge fight with Mom, and as I got upstairs the storm really
started. I didn't turn on any lights. It was nice. My window opens out
onto the kitchen roof, so I crawled out of it in my nightie and got soaking wet. I cried so hard that I was laughing, and the sky cracked with
jagged lightning, and I felt so small and exhilarated, and the tension
from my fight with Mom disappeared.

After I dried off I got in bed and called Sam, still on my natural rain-storm high, and told him how I'd fought with Mom because she thought the Miranda July movie I was watching was "morally repugnant" and "obscene," and made me turn it off. And I told him how since it had been so hot all the windows of our house were open and I could hear the rain so loud like an avalanche of glass beads. And it smelled so fresh and tasted so sweet.

Standing in the rain I thought about everything that has happened over the last year, remembering things in split-second visions like a TV high-light reel. About my art show, and how prom is in two days, and how it's going to be June tomorrow, which is when I told Roxie I'd wait until to have sex. And I have. And I still want to do it. Last Friday night Sam and I were on my couch, in the dark. Mom and Dad had gone upstairs to sleep. We straddled each other and pressed hard, gasping and grinding and making out. And we could've done it, but we didn't, even though soon it'll be "allowed," I guess.

For the past few weeks, I have been happy.

Friday, June 8, 5:58 p.m.

Okay.

It's almost dinnertime and I'm tired, but it's time to write about the **PROM FIASCO.** It's been almost a week and I think I'm finally ready to revisit what happened. I don't even know where to start. I'm nervous about even writing this down in case Mom happens to find it. I barely want to think about it. But here goes.

Prom was on Saturday. I finished my dress and it is an absolute DREAM! I love it so much.

PROM outfit

← HAIR IN SPECIAL BUN

FLOWER CLIP

mom's GLITTERY NECKLACE

RED LIPSTICK

MATCHING BRACELET

VINTAGE CLUTCH ROXIE GAVE ME

CUSTOM-MADE DRESS

RED HEELS BORROWED FROM NORA'S mom

How perfect my outfit was almost makes everything that happened worse, because it feels like it was all a waste.

Sam came to pick me up in his parents' car. Mom took pictures of us that will probably be shitty because she always forgets to turn off the flash.

Sam looked SO amazing in his tux. He got a pink tie and pocket square to match my dress and brought me a beautiful corsage with pink flowers and an orchid for my wrist. He smiled when he saw me and said,

"You look nice," but it was in that kind of squeaky fake voice that he does in front of Mom and Dad. I wish they weren't there so I could have gotten a real reaction and a real kiss.

We went to dinner at D'Anna's, which was super nice. Tim, Jenna, Annie, and Nathan were there too—we had reserved a big table and it felt so grown up. Everyone was looking at us because we were dressed up fancy.

We were walking over to Mallard to get ice cream after dinner when Roxie called me. She was in town to see her boyfriend and wanted to meet up while we were downtown so she could get a picture of us and see my dress and say hi. She met up with us on Railroad Ave. and took a photo of all of us with our dates. Then she said:

DO YOU GUYS WANT SOME WEED COOKIES TO EAT FOR THE DANCE?

She had made them a few days ago, and we said yes because all of us had been talking about how it would be fun to smoke or get a little drunk before the dance, but Annie, our main source, hadn't had any luck scoring booze, and we didn't know where we could smoke weed near the Yacht Club (where the prom was) without getting caught, and Sam is super nervous about doing stuff like that at school things because he's such a good student. Roxie gave us three weed cookies, one for each couple to split.

Jenna and Tim are both minorly stonerish and Annie and Nathan have smoked a TON, and they said that edibles were really fun and mellow and a perfect way to have a good time tonight without the smell of weed smoke or anything giving us away. We ate them before we had our ice cream and they were good. I had expected them to taste weed-y and skunk-ular, but they were almost like normal cookies.

We got our ice cream and wandered around downtown, linking arms and pretending we were fancy couples from an old movie, before heading to the prom. None of us felt anything close to high and we figured the cookies hadn't worked, which was fine, because they'd been kind of a last-minute thing anyway, so after rambling a bit more we finally went to the dance.

381

We had just gotten into the car to head to prom when Roxie called me.

She said that her boyfriend had just eaten some, and that they were super strong and she didn't want us to have them after all.

"It's too late, we already ate them," I said, "but all of us are feeling fine, not even high at all."

I told everyone what she'd said, but they didn't seem too concerned. "They probably had more than we did," Nathan said. "It affects everyone in different ways." And Annie said, "She's being paranoid—I've had brownies before and it's always fine. It's not like we just dropped acid or some shit."

When we got to the Yacht Club, we still felt fine, so we went inside. Then, it was so weird, the second we entered the building, I looked over at Sam, and I could tell that it hit us both at the exact same time. All of a sudden, we were so high. We gave each other a dread-filled look, and it was like everything around us became distorted and slowed down.

We had to walk past the principal, the vice principal, and a bunch of other teachers and chaperones who were standing and taking everyone's tickets under one of those balloon arches. They all wanted to say hi and talk to Sam because he's their favorite student, and tell us how nice we looked, and I felt hysterical, like we had to escape because if they talked to us for long enough, they'd know what was going on. I have no idea what we even said. All I could think was that I had to act as normal as possible and just get through the door without arousing suspicion... which somehow, we did. But I could tell Sam was totally falling apart next to me. He was so scared we were going to get caught.

Inside the dance, the music was loud. There were people everywhere and chocolate fountains with fruit and cake and stuff you could dip into them.

I WAS SO OVERWHELMED...

MY EYES FELT LIKE THEY WERE MOVING THROUGH **JELL-O,** LIKE I COULD SEE SLOW-MOTION **ECHOES** REVERBERATING OFF EVERY TINY MOVEMENT MY BODY MADE. THEY FELT HEAVY AND HARD TO KEEP OPEN, BUT ALSO LIKE I COULDN'T BLINK.

Sam was even further gone than I was, I could tell. And I was barely keeping it together! I was trying hard to make conversation with him and other people, so as not to arouse suspicion, because I'm pretty sure we were just standing in the middle of the room stunned.

We attempted to dance for a bit. The bass in the music made my head feel like a vibrating gong. Everything was spinning. I kept feeling like I couldn't see but was also hyperfocused on every tiny detail of everything around me. I saw Annie and Jenna dancing and they seemed totally unfazed. Jenna caught my eye and smiled a blissed-out stoner smile that told me she was in a totally different world than Sam and me. Asher Wilson was in the crowd, dancing with his date, Sarah Sokolowski. He was wearing a powder-blue vintage tuxedo and bolo tie with Converse high-tops, and Sarah was wearing a 60s mod minidress, and they were dancing totally different than everyone else. Just going wild, however they wanted, separate but together, jumping up and down, head-banging, twirling, shaking, and doing amazing disco moves. I couldn't help but stare. They looked like they were having so much fun. Like they were free from whatever weird show all the rest of us were putting on. It made me feel even more miserable and alone. I was grinding with Sam, trying to look normal and sober and like everyone else. And they were having the best time being different. I had a weird swell of jealousy so intense it made me feel sick. I just kept thinking that the way they were dancing was the way everyone ACTUALLY wants to dance but isn't brave enough to.

I don't know how long we were dancing, if you could call it that, because I think it was really me just slightly moving back and forth while Sam held on to me for dear life so he didn't pass out.

I started to feel sicker and made Sam sit down so he wouldn't fall over or get lost, and I went to the bathroom because I thought I was going to throw up or majorly freak out.

I was so upset. It was my first dance, my first PROM, and I had ruined it by eating a damn weed cookie that made me feel like shit. I just stared at myself in the mirror, and I looked so distorted and strange.

I KEPT FEELING LIKE MY FACE WAS SOMEONE ELSE'S, AND IT WOULD SCARE ME, BUT I COULDN'T LOOK AWAY.

At some point Annie and Jenna came in, because I remember Jenna saying, "You good?" and I said, "No." Then Annie said, "Awww, baby Phoebe's first time taking edibles!!!!" and laughed and I felt so mad that she didn't realize how seriously bad I felt.

Jenna looked worried but I could tell she was super stoned too, not like I was, but enough that she didn't know how to help. She kept saying, "Oh no!!" in a worried way but then laughing hysterically. They said Sam was glued to his chair, afraid to move in case he did something that looked "on drugs." "We're gonna go back out, come with us! It will feel better than just tripping out in here," Annie said, but I couldn't. I wanted to just stay in the bathroom until I felt like myself again. I could tell they felt about me like I had felt about Nora at the lake party, like they were checking on me just to be nice but really were annoyed that I was such a weed baby and was having a bad time. They were a fun high, and I didn't want to ruin their night by being needy and not okay. I could tell they really didn't WANT to know how bad I felt. They wanted to dance and have a good time, and I was supposed to be doing that with them. I'd made my dress specially and everything had been so perfect, and now it had all gone to shit.

I don't know how long I was in the bathroom—it could have been hours. After a while I went into a stall—the idea of going back onto the crowded dance floor made my head spin.

But I knew I couldn't stay in there forever. So finally I got up the courage to walk out. Asher Wilson was standing there, by the coatroom, like he was waiting for me. Once again, I'm running into him outside a bathroom, like at Jenna's party in March. I think I just stared at him like a zombie.

I felt like I was in a nightmare where you can't run or scream and you're just frozen until you wake up. And so I started to cry.

He pulled me into the coatroom and shut the door. "Shhh, the teachers will know something is up," he said, and I said, "Is it obvious?" and he said, "I mean…you and Sam look super fucked up." He said he saw me basically just standing on the dance floor earlier, staring at him and looking like I was gonna keel over, and then I'd disappeared and he got worried I wasn't okay.

I told him about the weed cookies, and about how I was worried that Sam was majorly losing it and would give us away, and about how I'd made my dress and no one was even going to see it now, and about how if I went back out into the dance everyone would know we were stoned and we'd get caught, and how I felt like we were going to die of highness. I was so out of it—I was talking to him in a way we don't usually talk during class. Just babbling everything that came into my mind.

Then he put a hand on each of my shoulders and said, "Look. Your dress is cool as hell. You ARE beautiful. And this is a shitty night and that sucks. But you're gonna be okay. You need to call someone and have them come and pick you up, and then you need to eat a bunch of food and drink a bunch of water and go to sleep." And I said, "Have you ever felt like this before?" and he said, "Yes." "And you're okay now?" And he said, "Yes, I'm okay now."

EVERYTHING AROUND US LOOKED
BLURRY AND WARPED,
EXCEPT FOR TINY DETAILS RIGHT IN FRONT
OF MY FACE, LIKE WHEN YOU'RE FOCUSING
A FANCY CAMERA LENS ON SOMETHING
SUPER CLOSE-UP.

I FELT LIKE I WAS GETTING LOST IN
THE LITTLE GOLDEN REFLECTIONS ON
HIS WILD, SHAGGY HAIR, AND THE
CREASE OF CONCERN BETWEEN HIS
EYEBROWS, AND HIS EYES, WHICH WERE
SO SPARKLY AND BRIGHT.

AND THEN I KISSED HIM.
WHAT THE FUCK!

I don't know how long it lasted, but when I pulled away he looked so surprised. I've never seen him look surprised; he always looks like he knows exactly what's up. Then he took a deep breath and said, "Thank you. But that's not what should happen right now." And he had me find my coat and my clutch with my phone in it, and said, "Who do you want me to call?" and I said Roxie. I don't even remember him calling. But when he hung up, he said, "Here's what you're going to do. You're going to go get Sam and take him outside with you and try to look as normal as possible, and then your sister is gonna come and you're gonna go home and be all right."

"Okay," I said, because he sounded so authoritative, and it was such a relief to have someone who knew what to do.

Shit—Mom is calling me to eat. I'll write more later.

10:19 p.m.

So, I wasn't aware of my body walking out of the coatroom and over to the table where Sam was sitting, but I know I did it somehow because all of a sudden, I was there. I took his hand and I said, "We need to go," and he just said, "Okay," and he looked so scared that it made me want to cry, because I think however high I was, he was higher—and flipping out hard.

I don't remember walking out, but we must have looked normal enough because no one questioned why we were leaving early. The next thing I remember was waiting outside for Roxie for what felt like 239493048 years. I remember seeing Asher and Sarah smoking on the hood of her car, and I could tell he was watching us, that maybe he'd even come out to smoke because he wanted to make sure we got out and got our ride. I wonder if he told Sarah what was going on, and that I'd kissed him in the coatroom because I was so stoned and just grateful that he was there.

Roxie finally arrived in her boyfriend's old blue Mercedes. She was freaking out because she felt so bad and was so upset that this was all her fault.

We ended up just sitting in the parking lot of the Yacht Club all night—I had this idea that we could take a break and sober up and be okay and go back in, but we sat for hours and only felt worse. We could hear the music from inside, and I hated knowing that we were missing it all. But it felt sadder to leave it behind and give up. Sam was flipping out in a major way. He was talking paranoid garbled gibberish in this chirpy, high-pitched voice and singing little songs and laughing hysterically, and even though I was super stoned too I just couldn't fathom that he couldn't get it together enough to shut up. I was alternating between being super annoyed with him and being super worried that he was never going to be okay, that he'd been broken somehow.

I know it was only a few hours that we were there, but it felt unbearable and so endless, and I didn't want to leave. Leaving felt like admitting defeat. We knew it was over when everyone came out, shouting and laughing, and started to drive away. And then Roxie started the car and said, "Sam, we have to get you home. Do you think you can get it together?" "...Yes...okay," Sam said meekly. We decided to risk Sam being a little late for his curfew and drove around town trying to get Sam to come down. I started to feel better, still really high but a more normal stoned now. But Sam was not coming down. Finally Roxie decided she had to take him back, otherwise his parents would really start to worry.

She was pissed, I could tell. Annoyed at having to deal with his loopiness all night, and I think just so mad at herself that any of this had happened.

Sam's dad must have been waiting up, because when we got to their house, his dad came right outside.

Sam opened his door, and the second he did, he threw up all over the driveway, and then I threw up too and started to cry.

Roxie told me the next day that she said we had eaten edibles, because she thought it was better to tell the truth about what we'd eaten, but that she'd lied and said she didn't know where we'd gotten them because she didn't want to get in trouble. She told Sam's dad she'd come and picked us up and made sure we were okay.

Sam's dad is kind of strict and intense, and I was so scared of what he was going to say. But Roxie said all he said to Sam was, "Well, you probably won't do this again, will you?" And thanked her for bringing him home.

Roxie brought me home and helped me take my prom things off, and put on my oldest, most tattered nightgown. We slept together in her bed, and I cried and cried, and she did too because she felt so bad, and she was so scared that she would get in trouble for giving us the cookies. Then I fell into a strange deep sleep where I know I had wild dreams but can't remember what they were. And now my hand is going to fall off because this entry was so long. And I'm falling asleep. I'll write more tomorrow.

Saturday, June 9, 11:22 a.m.

Okay. Basically, the next day, I was STILL STONED. Only a little bit, but it took me until the next night to feel totally normal again. I called Sam to make sure he was okay, and he said he was still feeling a little high, but better, and that his parents weren't mad, just thought he'd been immature. He said he'd asked them not to tell my parents about any of it, and they agreed. Which I can't BELIEVE. I just know that if Mom ever found out, she'd personally march both Roxie and me to the county jail.

I called everyone else in our group, because Roxie was so worried that they'd tell their parents or that they'd gotten into accidents and not been okay. Annie and Nathan said they'd gotten a little high and it had been fun, not in the same universe as how it had been for us. I was so relieved and also jealous. All of them said they wouldn't say it was Roxie who had given them the cookies if anyone asked. I don't know why Sam and I had such a wack reaction—I guess because we're the least experienced of the group with smoking pot, so we must have a low tolerance or something.

The worst part of being high on the next day was that we had to go to a family dinner at Grandma and Grandpa's, and it was so hard to concentrate and function like everything was totally normal. And since Grandma had helped me with my dress, she wanted to hear all about it. Everyone wanted a full report, and I just had to straight-up lie and be really vague about how it had been. Luckily Roxie was there and could help cover for me. Somehow, I don't think Mom and Dad suspect a thing.

I haven't talked to Sam much in the last few days. I checked in after it all went down, but since then he hasn't been texting me back very much, probably because we're in finals at school and he's always being so studious.

I feel like he wants to pretend like the whole thing didn't happen. I know I'm just freaking out for no reason, but I'm worried he's angry at me and resents that we ate weed cookies and missed our prom. I feel so guilty, like it was my fault, like I tricked him into eating the weed cookies even though I know that wasn't the case. And so guilty that when he was high, I just felt annoyed. I just wanted him to shut up and go away. I feel like he somehow knows what happened with Asher, that I accidentally told him when I was high or something, and that he is waiting for me to admit it to see how long I'm willing to live a lie. Maybe someone saw Asher and me come out of the coatroom, and told him, and he thinks I'm some kind of loose, drugged-out woman. Which I am. I cheated. I'm a cheater.

I feel so bad that Sam was sitting out alone at the dance, anxious and high and losing his shit, while I was off kissing another man.

I keep telling myself it was okay because I was out of it and didn't really know what I was doing. But then I worry that that's just some kind of excuse. Like, yes, I was super stoned, but am I using that to justify kissing Asher and not have it mean anything later??

It all just feels like such a muddled blur.

I REMEMBER SEEING HIS LIPS, AND WONDERING WHAT IT WOULD FEEL LIKE TO PUT MINE ON THEM, IF IT WOULD FEEL DIFFERENT OR THE SAME AS IT DOES WITH SAM. AND THEN SUDDENLY, I WAS KISSING HIM. LIKE THE WALL BETWEEN MY IMAGINATION AND REALITY HAD TUMBLED DOWN.

It was like this one Thanksgiving, when I was nine, and I was staring at one of Mom's perfect pumpkin pies on the counter, and I was overcome with a powerful urge to stick my finger right in the middle, feel it sink through the thick, pumpkin-y filling. And then before I knew it, I had, and Mom got so upset.

Sam is the only boy I've kissed, after all. (Well, not anymore.) And Asher was being so nice and making me feel so safe, and I guess I just felt overcome with gratefulness, and maybe confused about who he was, and was just being impulsive, I guess....But I know it was wrong, and I'm so scared of hurting Sam. And the worst part is that I know I have. Whether he ever finds out or not.

I can't stop wondering what Asher thought of the whole thing. He texted me late that night, asking if I got home okay. I didn't see it till morning, and just texted back, "Yeah. Thanks." I feel so embarrassed. I bet he thinks I'm such a weird, immature baby who can't even get stoned without crying and kissing random guys.

The Monday after prom he said hi to me like normal but then kind of avoided me all class. The yearbook is done since the year is almost over—they're off being printed. Prom was the last thing the staff covered. So, Mrs. Lynn pretty much lets us do whatever we want during class these days. Asher went into the back workroom to "clean up old files" on the computer and had big headphones on, probably playing loud music, so it was clear he didn't want to be bugged. And every other day he left right after Mrs. Lynn took attendance.

Maybe he told Sarah I kissed him and she banned him from interacting with me. Or she broke up with him and he's mad at me because it's my fault, and he wishes he hadn't helped me at all.

I just want things to be normal again. I don't know if I'm going to tell Sam that I kissed Asher. I think not. I feel like telling him will make it into something more serious than it was. Because it wasn't serious—I was just really high. It's not like I have feelings for Asher that are some kind of threat to Sam, so I think telling him would only weird him out and make him suspicious that I do. But it feels horrible having a secret. Like there's a little ball of acid in my chest that's going to slowly burn through and explode.

Monday, June 11, 4:55 p.m.

I'm feeling better than I was. Things are more back to normal after prom. I think the one thing I feel saddest about is my dress. I was just so excited to show it off, and I barely got the chance. And just missing the dance in general, it feels like such a rite of passage that is gone forever now. Roxie keeps trying to make me feel better, I think because she still feels bad. She said, "You're only a sophomore, so you'll get to go two more times." But I said, "Only if I'm asked," because it's hard to believe Sam would ever want to go with me again.

I hung out with him on Saturday night, which made things feel better again. It was nice to see him while we weren't high and remember that he's not annoying and that I love him and love us and am so relieved that we got through that night.

We went on a long walk around his neighborhood in the rain and then watched *The West Wing* (with which he and his whole family are obsessed—they own all the seasons on DVD) and ate take-out Casa Que Pasa potato burritos. Then after his family went to sleep, we kissed and kissed in the dark on his couch. It felt so good.

I said yes. That I was just tired. I didn't want the night to end. I wanted to just keep soaking up time with Sam to remind myself that being with him, kissing him, feels more right than kissing Asher ever could.

I hate always being on a couch or stealing limited time in one of our beds. I wish we had a place to go, where we could just BE together, no holds barred. I never want to feel out of my mind like I did when we were high again. I hated that it made me annoyed with him.

School ends in ten days. And Mom is cooking lamb and feta pasta for dinner. And I don't have very many pages left in this book. And my nails need clipping—I need to stop biting them off. I'm excited for summer to come, but...

I wish Hanley was doing another summer play this year, so I'd be guaranteed to see Sam every day. I'm worried he'll find some way to be working and studying all the time even in the summer. Lukas Viitala is selling Sam his silver Saab! For only $1. Apparently Lukas bought it for a dollar from a senior last year, and so it's a tradition now. He's going to UW in the fall, and Mari is going far away to Ithaca, in New York, to study music.

It's going to be so weird without them here next year.

I saw Asher today in Yearbook class but things were still weird. My heart beats so fast every time I see him now, even though it's not as if it's some kind of surprise that he's there. Today he did what he did all last week, said hi then waited till attendance was over and either worked alone or left. I feel so sad, like not only have I tainted the relationship I'm in with Sam, whether he ever finds out or not, but like I've also ruined Asher's and my friendship, which I think I didn't even realize I cared about so much. Besides Mari, and sometimes Nora, he felt like the one person I could really be myself around. Like I can kind of be around Sam—but I get more caught up thinking about how I look or seem with him. Whereas with Asher things just feel...effortless. How easy would it have been for me not to just randomly kiss him when I was high??? Why couldn't I control myself for that one tiny second? Now everything has changed. I don't know if he's going to keep ignoring me all week. I don't even know what I'd want him to say. Maybe I need to say something first, since I'm the one who kissed him, after all. He would have a right to be mad at me since I'm the one who went in for the ill-fated, adulterous kiss. Sigh. I want school to be over already so all of this will go away.

Tuesday, June 12, 5:23 p.m.

I told Mari about what happened with Asher after prom when we were walking home from school together today. I'd already told her about the weed-cookies debacle, but had left out all the parts with Asher in them because I felt like saying it out loud to someone would make it more real that I cheated on Sam. When I told her about the kiss, she just nodded slowly and said, "I'm kind of not surprised. It always seems like there's something going on between you two." Which rattled me to the core, because if she thinks that, what if other people do too?? What if Sam does? "What do you mean??" I said, and she said that she's seen us before after school or during Yearbook when we're walking around the school taking photos and stuff.

YOU'RE BOTH JUST ALWAYS SMILING AND LAUGHING WHEN YOU'RE AROUND EACH OTHER. AND YOU TALK ABOUT HIM A LOT. JUST KIND OF CASUALLY.

I DO??

Then she said something that caught me totally off guard. She said, "Did you know that Nora asked if he would take her to prom?" I think my jaw dropped like some kind of cartoon. I had no idea. I mean, I knew she liked him ages ago, but she says so little about that kind of thing and didn't let anything on when I talked to her about prom. And how had Asher not told me??

"He said no of course, since he was going with Sarah."

It made me extra glad I'd chosen to tell Mari about kissing him, and not Nora. Even though she doesn't know what happened, the whole thing makes me feel even guiltier about the kiss.

Mari asked if I was going to tell Sam, and I said no. "I don't want him to think it's a THING. Like something he needs to worry about." Mari nodded and was quiet for a minute, and then said, "So there isn't anything for him to worry about?" which made me annoyed. "NO! It's not like I did it on purpose—I wasn't in my right mind." I thought Mari would be the least judgy, but here she was making me feel guilty, as if I intentionally committed adultery against Sam! Like I'm harboring some secret love for Asher. Which I'm not. If anything…it's just a weird fascination sometimes, like I find my mind moving toward him whenever it's idle. When I'm deep in a painting or out on a walk, or in that moment in the dark right before you fall asleep. It's then that I remember the softness of the kiss, and his sparkling eyes and the crease of concern on his forehead, and the way he made me feel safe in a blur of confusion and weirdness.

Maybe Mari is right. Maybe there is something for Sam to worry about. I hate myself for thinking and feeling these things.

Wednesday, June 13, 8:44 p.m.

I went thrifting with Nora after school today. We talked about what plays we hope Hanley picks for the fall—Nora wants Shakespeare, I want another fun, campy farce like *Tom Jones*.

At Value Village we scored some amazing finds, the best of which was TWO MATCHING vintage plasticky airline shoulder bags. We want to do a little photoshoot with them where we dress up like 60s stewardesses.

P.S.

It's almost warm enough out to swim!!!

VINTAGE AIRLINE BAGS!!

INCREDIBLE GREEN 60s DRESS

COOL WOOL COAT THAT NORA FOUND

Thursday, June 14, ? p.m.

Asher finally broke his silence today. Or I forced him to. We didn't talk about the kiss, but at least the cold-shoulder-ness between us is gone. I decided that I was just going to go back to being friendly and normal, just start interacting again because Yearbook periods have been so tense, and I don't want things to be left weird at the end of the year. And I don't want to prove Mari's and my fears right that there is something between us. I want it to be comfortable and goofy again.

He was outside the Yearbook room on the lawn, lying out in the sun, so I just went over and sat down. The grass is covered in those tiny miniature pinky-white daisies right now, so I put one on his forehead. He opened his eyes and said, "'Ey!" then blew the daisy off and sat up.

I had been worried things would be awkward, because maybe he just wants to be done being friends. Maybe he was mad or annoyed at me for kissing him or ruining his prom night by being so high and out of it and needing help. But then he grinned, and then he was just the same old friendly but inscrutable Asher. Maybe the beautiful summery weather and school almost being out made him just want to put things aside.

Since there wasn't anything to do we just sat in the grass outside the

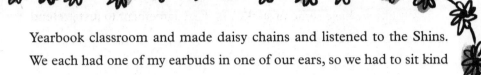

Yearbook classroom and made daisy chains and listened to the Shins. We each had one of my earbuds in one of our ears, so we had to sit kind of close.

We didn't talk about prom. We actually barely talked at all, but it still felt so good to be silent in a friendly way. He made a daisy crown for his wild hair, and a daisy necklace, and even dangled some off his ears.

I died laughing and got a picture on my Polaroid, and then he took one of me.

It felt like we have some unspoken mutual agreement to just pretend like prom didn't happen, which I'm glad of, but it also feels a little weird, because I can't help but wonder what he thinks of it now. Maybe he's kissed so many people that it just isn't as big of a deal to him. Annie did tell me he's been with a lot of girls, after all.

Friday, June 15, 10:42 p.m.

I have started driver's ed. It's boring. I really don't want to talk about it. It's hot and we sit in this small room in a strip mall and listen to a guy who seems like he's probably a Republican talk, and watch ancient safety videos from like 1979.

Roxie comes home Saturday for her tonsillectomy, and she'll be here for a long time. I'm excited for her to be home but also annoyed because it means I'll have less time to be alone with Sam when Mom and Dad aren't home. And even though she says she doesn't hate Sam I feel like she secretly does. She thinks he's annoying, especially after seeing him so high, and probably thinks he's the one coercing me into sex even though I'm the one who brought it up first.

He came over today and it was nice. We were pretty much naked but again we didn't do "it." And that's fine. I have this feeling that we'll know when the right time to do "it" is. We held each other tight, and it was so warm there, wrapped up in him. So comfortable. I do feel like "it" is coming closer, though. It's nice that we could do it anytime but we haven't. It makes me feel mature.

I'm worried I won't see anyone over the summer because there's no play, and everyone is going on trips or getting ready for college. But I have to remember that they're my friends now, and we hang out whether we're in a show or not. At least until some of them leave.

I'm going to be starting a job at a plant nursery down the street in mid-July, weeding and watering and doing gardeny kinds of tasks. I'm excited but also annoyed that I'll have to be somewhere at a certain time when summer is supposed to be all lazing about reading in the yard and swimming and sleeping in....

I'm having a sucky day. Mostly because I have to deal with Mom and Dad, and am grumpy and don't want to deal with driver's ed. I don't even care that much about getting my license since Sam has the Saab. I just want to fast-forward a week till we're all out of school and it's officially summer break!

MONDAY, JUNE 18, 6:11 P.M.

It's the last week of school, which feels both exciting and sad. Last year I was only excited to be done, I think because I didn't have friends like I do now.

We have been playing games in the Little Theater during drama class and helping Hanley clean out the costume and prop closets, which have turned to utter chaos after two semesters of classes and the play.

After class today, I left a letter on her desk. I've been wanting to let her know how grateful I am that she encouraged me to try out for the summer play last year. Without her encouragement I wouldn't be friends with anyone I'm friends with now, and I definitely wouldn't have met Sam.

I felt shy about giving it to her when she was there, so I left it on her desk and ran away, since this week is my last chance before school ends.

Here is what my letter said:

To Vicki Hanley, A THANK-YOU NOTE.

It was a scheduling mistake that I was ever in drama class last year. I didn't want to be, though everyone around me seemed to think it was a good idea. In fact, I dreaded it. Getting up on a stage in front of people I didn't know just last year seemed like an absolutely terrible thought, burdened as I was by insecurity and self-consciousness, traits commonly found in those Lilliputians known as freshmen. "Drama wasn't my thing," I had tried vainly to convince myself. Because the truth of it was, I was in denial.

It had been years since I'd been onstage. The only acting I'd done had been at children's theater camp, which however sloppy had given me a small taste of the thing that I had been so desperately (and secretly) longing for as a high school freshman—the stage.

So, as I stared down at my schedule, looking at the words "Drama 1" and the ever-so-sinister name of "V. Hanley," waves of both fear and euphoria swept through me. I was afraid to act, because I knew that if I did, I might never be able to stop, that I'd get sucked into that mysterious crowd of people known as the Thespians. That I would start memorizing Shakespeare for the pure fun of it and listen to the "Rent" soundtrack over and over and that I would become...dare I say...UNCOOL in the eyes of my peers. It was that tiny part of me, the part that embraced my inner drama nerd, that kept me in the class, that part that was searching to see if maybe there was an actor inside me. As the semester went on, I was still unconvinced of my Thespian-ocity. The drama games we played seemed to reduce my excitement to act, and the skits were just ploys to prove that there were better actors than I.

Then it was time for our final monologues. All I can say is that my knees knocked just thinking about it, and other than that I won't elaborate on my fear. I remember before I was about to go onstage, feeling as if I wanted to scream and laugh and throw up. I was shaking all over.

But none of that stopped me from standing up and saying, "I'll go next."

I remember watching my feet mount the stage steps and thinking, "This is it." Thinking of the myriad things I could do at that moment (running away seemed the most appealing), but I chose to go on with the show, and I channeled every feeling and emotion rushing through my body until they became the emotions of someone else. As I sat down in my chair, the spotlight on me, I looked out to the audience of restless teenagers, and I felt the buzzing energy all around me. And I knew in the split second before I opened my mouth and delivered the monologue I had carelessly chosen out of many others that I was an actor. When I finished, in the small silence before everyone clapped, I felt so utterly free and happy, and I wanted to cry. And I almost did. I almost cried when I walked down the steps, shaking and shivering, and I went to talk to you, and you asked me where I'd been. Where I'd been hiding. I'd been hiding there, in the theater, the whole time. You hadn't known it, and neither had I, but what I do know is that you, Vicki Hanley, have changed my life forever, and I would not be the person I am today without you.

Thank you for everything.

Love, PHOEBE

Thursday, June 21, 5:33 p.m.

School ended today!!! It was an early release, and at 11 a.m., when the last bell rang, everyone poured out of their classrooms and cheered and hugged and a lot of seniors cried. The whole crew met up in the drama room and Ms. Hanley cried about Lukas and Mari and Annie leaving, and we all gathered on the Little Theater stage and held hands in a circle, and

then I started crying too, a bunch of people did, because it's so hard to imagine what drama is going to be like without them.

It was the most beautiful day, warm and sunny, and Sam and I drove to my house to hang out in the yard before he had to work at the Toy Jungle. We made a kind of fort out of quilts and blankets on the clothesline and cuddled inside it kissing and touching and holding each other close.

I could feel this intense, force-tastic, in-sync kind of energy between us, like we were both so hungry for more, ready for more, like this question mark, this idea of whether we would have sex that's felt like it's been hovering between us, just out of focus, was starting to get crisp and clear. Starting to feel closer, and less scary and more real.

WE SAID WE'D WAIT TILL JUNE, RIGHT? TO HAVE SEX?

IT FELT SO GOOD TO HEAR HIM BRING IT UP. TO FINALLY NOT BE THE ONLY ONE ASKING WHEN HE THOUGHT THE TIME WOULD COME. MY HEART SKIPPED A BEAT, AND I SAID, YES.

Then he said, "Well, we're gonna have to do it soon, then, because soon it'll be July," and I thought I'd faint with happiness. Because it's not as if it's the sex itself I've been so excited to experience—it almost felt more important to just hear him initiate and indicate that he wants to do it with ME. That he loves ME and wants to make that love physical and tangible and real with ME.

I wished we could have done it then and there, but Mom was home so we couldn't go inside, and I wasn't about to lose my virginity in broad daylight in the backyard. It would be just my luck that some neighbor would come by and be scandalized and ruin my life. Plus, he had to work at 4, and do family stuff tonight, and we didn't want it to be rushed.

We decided that tomorrow would be a perfect day. School was over, and miraculously we both had no plans. AND since it was a weekday, his parents would be gone at work all day and his sister was going to horse camp, so we'd have his house all to ourselves. My heart was racing just planning it. I felt this wild, ecstatic energy running through me that made me want to get up and shake my body around and laugh. It just felt so surreal that it was finally going to be a thing. I could tell Sam was happy too, and that both of us were finally ready, and that it finally wouldn't feel rushed, now that school is over, and we've been together so long.

We ate raspberries and snap peas from the garden and read to each other from *A Midsummer Night's Dream*, which Sam has been reading for fun (of course he would read Shakespeare for FUN), and it was just so amazingly lovely and nice, knowing that we were both feeling and wanting the same things, knowing that I wasn't just some lone, wayward woman in our relationship anymore, the only one who thought about sex, and that this was something we were planning and deciding as one. It felt like there was a glowing thread connecting our hearts, sparking and pulsing and all our own.

When he left for work, he gave me the most delicious goodbye kiss.

I was so happy afterward that I even played Bananagrams with Mom and drank iced tea at the picnic table, which she's always trying to get me to do.

Sigh. I am perfectly content.

SATURDAY, JUNE 23, 5:02 A.M.

I can't even begin to know where I should start with everything that happened yesterday. And it really feels like it was today, because it's so early and I've gotten so little sleep, so it feels like it's just been one long, amazing, weird, and terrible day. I'm exhausted and scatterbrained and feeling utterly overwhelmed and it's the crack of dawn, but I don't know if I can go back to sleep, and so I think I'll probably feel better if I just write.

I guess I should start with the fact that Auntie Eve died. But I don't really want to. There's just been so much going on. The long and short of it is, she had a stroke. We have to go to Florida tomorrow, for the service, and then stay for at least a week to clear out all the crap from her house.

But that's not what I want to start with.

WHAT I REALLY WANT TO START WITH... IS THAT

I LOST MY VIRGINITY.

It was at Sam's house. I went over there yesterday morning, although it feels like a lifetime ago. It was the most beautiful, perfect summer morning, the kind that's the most perfect balmy temperature before the clouds burn off and it gets really hot. We moseyed around his neighborhood and then lay on the trampoline in his yard, like we did one of the first times he fingered me in the fall. But this time we didn't need blankets or coats or our hands down each other's pants to keep us warm.

Then we went inside, and...it just happened. Well, we talked more about it first. Because even though I've been wanting to do it for so long, I got nervous once we were naked in his bed, and a little scared, and so we just held each other and talked about where we were, how things had been, and where we were going, and by the time we were done, we were ready.

We used protection of course. A red condom from the bunch that he'd bought back in January. I knew it might be painful, and when he went in there was a kind of pop feeling, and I cried out because it really did hurt, but it only lasted a second, and Sam was gentle and slow.

And after that, it just felt funny, like I imagined it would, I guess, like there was something in my vagina moving in and out, which there was. But there wasn't anything that felt more special or mysterious than that, really. It didn't last long, which I didn't mind, and I know the first time is always weird and that it will get better. Roxie built it up to be something so scary and painful but it really wasn't that bad. And I had psyched it up to be such a big, sweeping, romantic, life-changing thing, and it's not that it wasn't romantic. It was nice.

But it felt very small, and intimate, and simple in a way. Afterward, I went to the bathroom and peed, because I read in *Cosmo* that you're supposed to pee after sex to avoid UTIs. And I looked in the mirror, and nothing was different.

I got back in bed and we kissed and kissed and held each other and napped in the warm sun like cats, and it was bliss.

I STILL LOOKED LIKE MYSELF... AND STILL FELT LIKE MYSELF.

Then we walked to the mini-mart and got sandwiches and had a picnic at Whatcom Falls Park and smoked a joint Roxie gave me in the tree house in Sam's backyard and kissed and held each other some more, laughing about how surreal it all felt.

After the joint we smoked wore off, we got in the car and drove to my house to pick up my swimsuit, because Jenna had texted us that the whole drama crew was gathering for a "school's out" swim day and campout at her house on the lake. As if the day couldn't get any more perfect! When we left his house it felt like coming out of Narnia into the real world. I'd almost forgotten that other people existed and that we wouldn't just be in a delicious loop of lovemaking and sandwich-eating and joint-smoking for the rest of time.

It's sooo nice now that Sam has the Saab and we don't always have to rely on our parents for rides!!! We picked up Mari and Lukas and Nora and Owen, and Sam offered to let Lukas drive, since it was so recently his car, but Lukas said, "This baby is yours now, you should do the honors." Mari, Nora, Owen, and I were all squeezed in the back, double-buckled, which normally would make Sam nervous as he's a stickler for rules, but I think he was too blissed-out to care. To think a year ago I would have just about fainted at being squished so close to Owen in a car.

I remember how those girls I met in Montana thought I'd lose my virginity to Owen at a music festival—and there I was sitting next to him having just lost it to Sam. It's just so weird that in the book of my life—the chapter about who I lose my virginity to and when has been written now. It's like I've been reading and reading and waiting to see what happens and all of a sudden I know. It's not a surprise anymore, and I'll never be able to unknow—I'll never have my first time again.

Annie and Jenna were already out on the dock and cheered when we arrived. We swam and ate corn chips and salsa and lay in the sun all afternoon and it was heavenly. Although I'm pretty sure I got a bad sunburn on my chest. Swimming is where my body feels most at home. I think I could float and tread water for days without even getting tired. I love how powerful yet featherlight I feel in the water. More graceful and strong than I ever feel on land. It was just so refreshing, and everyone was so happy to be done with school. The lake water was really warm from all the hot days we've had in the last week, and we did cannonball and handstand contests in the shallow water along the beach.

I was itching to tell the girls what we'd done earlier in the day, but there wasn't a good moment because we were in such a big group, and there was also something nice about having a delicious secret too. I always tell everyone everything right away, so it was a rare treat to be forced to keep it to myself. Like a little piece of magic between just Sam and me.

I kept catching his eye all evening and we would share a little smile, or I could just tell in his eyes that he was thinking about our morning too.

I WONDERED IF MARI AND THE OTHERS COULD TELL WHAT HAD HAPPENED. BECAUSE I DID FEEL A BIT LIKE A DOPEY, GIDDY GLOW WAS RADIATING OFF SAM AND ME, LIKE A NEON SIGN WAS HOVERING OVER OUR HEADS.

In the evening, David, Nathan, Tim, and Freya showed up with beers and boxed wine that Freya's older brother had bought. It was one of those perfect times with friends, where we were all so happy and relaxed. Even Nora drank some wine! Jenna's brother, Jack, ordered us pizzas and Annie flirted with him and got him to sneak us some more beer from his parents' pantry. I got a little drunk and smoked a spliff with Annie on the dock, and we put our feet in the water, and it felt so amazingly, deliciously warm.

We made a fire on the beach, and everyone gathered around it, drinking and laughing and reminiscing about the year and the plays and what things would be like in the fall. I noticed Lukas had his arm around

Mari, and Tim and Jenna kept sneaking away to make out. Sam kept holding my hand and kissing my cheeks and neck and hugging me tight, and he's usually so anti-PDA, but it just felt like everyone was in one big *Our Town* moment, like we were in a collective, blissful golden dream, and I never wanted it to end.

But it did.

Around midnight Jack came down onto the dock and yelled something we couldn't hear, so Jenna went over to talk to him. (Jenna's parents were gone for the weekend, so he was "in charge" of making sure we didn't get too wild.)

I knew immediately that something must be wrong because why else would she call Jenna's parents' house in the middle of the night—I checked to see if she'd been calling my cell but it was dead. I wished Sam would go with me to the house. But he was drunk and deep in conversation with Nathan, so I went on my own with Jack up to the house, where Asher and their friend Dylan were talking but went quiet when I walked in. Asher is friends with Jack, so I don't know why him being there surprised me, but for some reason it made my stomach jolt. I'd felt buzzed on the beach, but now I felt totally sober, like it was some kind of emergency and my body said, "This is not the time."

I picked up the phone, and that was when Mom told me about Auntie Eve. I don't even remember what I said. That I was sorry, I think. Mom was crying so hard, and it made me cry, not necessarily because I was sad about Auntie Eve dying, but something about hearing Mom cry just made me so upset. I could feel Jack and Asher and Dylan listening to me in a "trying not to listen" way.

I didn't really WANT to go home to a house of sadness, but it also felt wrong to stay. The magic golden bubble that had encompassed the whole day so far felt like it had popped.

I hung up and kind of stood there for a minute not knowing what to do. So, I just walked out and sat down on the grass in the yard. I could see everyone around the fire laughing and joking on the beach, but I felt numb, and overwhelmed, and not ready to go back and explain why I was suddenly sad.

Then someone came and sat next to me. It was Asher, and he said, "Hi," and I said, "Hey," and I hoped there wasn't any snot or mascara running down my face. Why is he always randomly around when I'm in the absolutely weirdest, most surreal and shit-tastic moments of my life? "My mom's sister died. That was my mom," I said. Because I realized I hadn't said what was going on, and he didn't know.

And we sat in silence for a minute.

Then all of a sudden, I felt so angry. And I know I'm going to sound like such an obnoxious, selfish bitch even writing this. I was angry and resentful that my mom had called with such bad news and completely ruined the party and my day that was supposed to be so perfect and momentous. I was angry at myself for resenting Mom when her sister had died and for being a narcissistic ass when I should be sad too. I was angry that it was Asher sitting next to me, and not Sam. Angry that Sam was drunk when I needed him, that he didn't somehow telepathically know that something was wrong and that he should sober up and come comfort me. I was angry that Asher has just been ignoring what happened at prom, like he's embarrassed, or forgot, or wants to just pretend it out of existence. I was angry that he was always AROUND just being nice when I needed him.

So, before I even had time to think twice about it I said, "Why haven't we talked about prom?" And I think it caught him off guard, because we'd been talking about my aunt, and he was silent for a minute, like he didn't know what to say.

Then he said, "What part of prom?" which really pissed me off. As if he didn't know what I was talking about.

"You know what fucking part," I said, and then I whispered because I was worried Sam could hear me from the beach. "I kissed you and we're acting like it just wasn't a thing."

And then I started to cry. It was the kind of crying where you open your mouth in a wail but it's completely quiet, like your whole inner body is contracting in silent agony. It was like the pain of hearing Mom so upset, and of cheating on Sam, and of having sex, which wasn't sad but just felt so big and REAL, was twisting together and forming a tornado inside me that had to get out. I wasn't looking at him. All I could think about was Sam only a stone's throw away and what a terrible girlfriend I was that I was even up here with Asher and not down there with him. I could see in the periphery of my vision that he had kind of put his arm out, like he wasn't sure if he should comfort me, but then he drew it back, not knowing what to do.

I GUESS... I WAS WAITING FOR YOU TO BRING IT UP FIRST... BECAUSE I DIDN'T KNOW IF YOU REMEMBERED IT.

And we were quiet, just sitting and listening to the sounds of the popping fire and people down by the lake. I could hear Sam and Nathan singing a Monty Python song. I felt like they were in a different world.

I didn't know what else to say, so silence fell again.

Then we heard a whooshing hiss and saw a cloud of steam and smoke rise from below, which meant that everyone had put the fire out, and sure enough their talking and laughter was getting closer as they came up the steps from the beach.

"Do you want a ride home?" Asher said as everyone approached. "Yes," I said quickly, because as soon as he'd said it, I'd felt relief at the thought. Even though Mom had said I should stay, it just felt too weird.

Sam came over and looked confused to see me so upset and sitting with Asher on the lawn.

"What was the call about?" he asked, and I stood up and told him and the others what my mom had said, and that I needed to go. Sam enveloped me into a big hug. It made me want to cry again, smelling his amazing, comforting scent. The morning we'd spent together felt so far away. But with that hug it all came rushing back, and I felt guilty for wanting to go. And jealous that everyone was going to keep hanging out without me, but I also knew I didn't want to stay. Everyone gave me hugs, and Sam gave me a long goodbye kiss, which he only does in front of people if he's really drunk, and he said, "I love you. Text me when you get home," and I couldn't believe that he'd said "I love you" in front of the group. I said I would, and that I was sorry, and that I loved him too. I gathered my stuff, and when we got into Asher's Subaru, he let me pick a CD, and I put on *The Moon & Antarctica* by Modest Mouse because I wanted to hear "Gravity Rides Everything."

The sunroof and windows were open, and the air was so summery and sweet. It reminded me of driving with Owen after *Thoreau* almost a year ago, except so much less awkward and strange. So much has changed since then, since I started this book.

While we drove, Asher was acting very un-Asher-y, making lots of small talk and telling me funny stories. I think he was trying to cheer me up and get me to laugh. We drove for a while, winding around the little road that goes along the lake, and then we came around a bend and Asher said, "Holy fuck." And I thought something was wrong, but then he said, "Do you see that moon?" and slowed down. I couldn't, so he pulled over by a little beach and we got out to take a look. It was huge and completely full, and glowing an incredible golden pink.

WE WENT QUIET AND I REALIZED IT WAS THE
FIRST TIME WE'D MADE EYE CONTACT ALL
NIGHT. AND JUST LIKE WHEN WE WERE IN
THAT COATROOM AT PROM, IT FELT LIKE WE
HAD ENTERED SOME OTHER WORLD, EVEN THOUGH
I WASN'T HIGH — IT WAS LIKE TIME HAD
STOPPED OR SLOWED DOWN.

Finally one of us broke eye contact, and it was like pulling away from a strong vacuum. And we just stared at the moon for a while. It was still so warm out, and the lake was perfectly still and bright, reflecting the moon's light. And then I did maybe the craziest thing I've ever done in my life. I said, "Do you want to swim?" because it just…felt like the right thing to do. It was like someone else had spoken through my body, and I almost surprised myself. Asher looked at me and said, "Yes." And so at the exact same time, we ran toward the beach, and stripped off our clothes as fast as we could, and jumped into the lake in our underwear.

We screamed and laughed hysterically and could hear it echoing across the water.

We swam out to where our feet couldn't touch. The water was perfectly warm, even though the sun was long gone. Then I asked what I'd wanted to ask back at Jenna's before he offered me a ride. I said, "So… you don't want anything from me?" about what he'd said about our kiss.

He gave me a long look, then smiled his smirky smile, like he was going to laugh, but when he spoke, he sounded more serious than I'd ever heard him be.

443

NOT "NO" OR "I DON'T LIKE YOU LIKE THAT," JUST... "YOU HAVE A BOYFRIEND."

So I said, "You have Sarah too, right?" because it annoys me that he never brings her up, and that in this moment the only thing he had to say was about MY relationship and not his.

"I—yeah. I did." He said, "Not anymore. Since she's graduating and all."

"Are you sad?" I asked, and he just said, "I've had other stuff on my mind."

We splashed around in silence for a while. A few times it felt like his foot brushed my thigh, or my shoulder would accidentally touch his and make my heart flip-flop with a flutter of adrenaline.

We swam to where our feet could just barely touch the lake bottom again. It was soft, smooth sand, not pebbly rock like on Jenna's beach, and we were standing on our tiptoes, our arms swishing the water around us. We were making eye contact again, and his hand caught mine and kind of lingered there.

THEN I SAID, I HAD SEX FOR THE FIRST TIME TODAY.

I don't even know why I said it. It was such a fucking weird thing tell him right then.

I had this feeling like I was on a cliff edge, about to fall off, and I had to say something out loud to pull myself back. To remind myself and him that Sam's and my relationship was still real, that we had something beautiful and momentous. Because I felt so...out to sea. Or out to lake, I should say. Like I was in a weird no-man's-land of time and space and needed to remember concrete things so that I wouldn't just drift away into this moonlight world with Asher and never find my way back. And I think some fucked-up part of me wanted to see his reaction too. Wanted to impress him or something.

Asher moved his hand away. He was looking right at me with a weird look on his face, which made sense because it had been SUCH a weird fucking thing to say. Then after a minute, he just said, "Cool," and turned around and swam toward the beach. In the moonlight I could see his wet boxer briefs clinging to his legs. It's funny how underwear is almost the exact same as swimsuits, but it somehow feels so much more intimate and taboo to be wearing it in front of someone. It's not like we were naked, or had kissed again, but I already felt that burning acid ball of guilt in my chest like I had after prom. I felt disappointed by his reaction, even though I don't know what I wanted him to say.

I got out of the water too, and I realized I hadn't felt at all self conscious of the way I looked until that moment. I tried not to care that my underwear was wet and see-through and that my hair was slicked back and strand-y. He found a blanket in the back of his car and gave it to me because I was shivering even though the air was so warm.

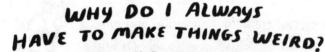

We drove to my house in silence, listening to Sufjan and dripping all over his car. I wished I hadn't made things weird. Why do I always have to make things weird?

All I said when I got home was "Thanks for the ride" and he said, "Anytime."

And I went inside and crawled into Mom and Dad's bed and started to cry so hard. And Mom woke up just enough to hold me and she cried

too. I know she was crying about Auntie Eve and thought I was too, but I didn't care. I just needed to cry.

It had started out as such an incredible day, but it had taken such an utterly strange and dreamlike turn. I wanted to wake Mom up and tell her everything, about how I'd lost my virginity today, and gotten stoned at prom, and kissed Asher, and swam with him in the moonlight, and about this terrible, boiling, burning guilt I feel inside. But I knew it wasn't the time, and that telling her those things would backfire in some way and probably get me in trouble, and so instead I just went to sleep, and only woke up and got in my own bed a few minutes ago.

I'm so exhausted and confused and am going to try to sleep again. I'll write more later.

4:44 p.m.

Today has been a weird day of packing and getting ready to go to Florida, which I can't wrap my brain around.

It feels like it's the same day as yesterday, since I got so little sleep, and so time just feels strange and endless and everything seems like a dream right now. I forgot to text Sam last night, so he called me today and asked how I was. I wanted to meet up with him so bad because it feels so wrong not to see him and kiss him and hold him and tell him everything that happened with Asher last night. But I know I need to help Mom get ready here, and even though it feels

horrible that he doesn't know, I don't know if I'll be able to tell him what I did.

I'm so frustrated that this happened now, and I feel guilty for being frustrated, since it's not like Auntie Eve chose when to die. I just had this idea that since it's summer it would be so relaxed, and we'd have ample time to bask in the new excitement of sex and hang out every day kissing in the sun and making love....

I hope Mom decides to be less of a bitch and lets me get away from packing to see him tonight. Doesn't she care that it's going to be about 45968098 years till we'll be together again?? And even if we can hang out, I know it will feel rushed, and we won't have time to really BE together.

I keep trying to go over the good parts of yesterday and bring them to the forefront of my memory instead of thinking about what happened with Asher last night, so that it can kind of record over the tape in my mind. Kissing Sam in his sunlit bed, picnicking and smoking a joint in the tree house, giddy with post-sex adrenaline, swimming and hanging out with everyone by the fire. Even though I know "recording over it" doesn't mean it didn't happen, I just feel gross every time my mind wanders to being with Asher in the lake. Touching hands. The silent drive home. And what it felt like to kiss him at prom, even if it was quick.

Sunday, June 24, ? P.M.

I'm on a plane. I hate being on planes. I don't know what time it is, because I'm in who knows what time zone on my way to Florida with Roxie, Mom, and Dad.

We flew over Mount Rainier poking through the clouds earlier—it was massive and looked like some sci-fi island in a sea of fluffy white.

Mom did end up letting me go see Sam last night. I feel bad that I called her a bitch. And that I went over to Sam's instead of helping when I know she was just barely keeping it together as we finished packing to leave for Florida today.

Anyway. We were able to hang out more INTIMATELY (without his parents and sister breathing down our necks) than I thought we would, which was nice. His family went upstairs to bed after we watched a movie, and Sam and I hung out in their den with the lights off, lying on the couch and holding each other in the dark. It was so nice to be close. I could hear his heart beating through his shirt, and the steady pace of it made me feel so comforted and safe.

He said, "I felt bad that I was too out of it and couldn't be the one to drive you home last night." My heart rate spiked when he said that, as if he somehow knew about my late-night swim session with Asher. I said it was okay, and that I was glad he got to stay and have fun. Even though now I wish he had been sober enough to drive me too, so that he could have saved me from myself and my utterly ill-advised and impulsive cheater-ly ways.

Then he said, "I didn't know you were such good friends with Asher." My heart really kicked into high gear then. I was worried he could feel it, since we were cuddled so close. I could feel that my face got red and hot too, and I was glad the lights were off at least. It felt like a deciding moment; should I do the mature thing and tell him the truth? Or protect him and lie, because what good would the truth do anyway? It would only be opening such a big can of worms right before I leave, making Sam upset at me right when he'd have ample time to stew on how terrible I am while I was gone. "Well, we hang out in Yearbook almost every day," I said, which wasn't a lie. "And he was just kind of there when I got off the phone and was sober and could drive me home." Which also wasn't a lie.

And him saying that broke my heart, and I started to cry. I cried and cried to him, letting out tears instead of the truth of everything that went on. It made the shame inside me feel a tiny bit relieved, even if I hadn't come clean. I told him that I loved him, and that I wanted only to be with him. Which isn't a lie. I DO love Sam, and I DO love being together. We kissed and kissed, and I nuzzled into his neck and smelled his comforting smell. He drove me home after that, and I got in bed and texted him about how much I was going to miss him to calm any lingering Asher-related guilt.

And now I'm on my way to Florida.

For lord knows how long. With limited cell reception. To hang out with Mom and Roxie and Dad and all the old hippies on Auntie Eve's commune in the woods. There's only a few more pages in this book, so I'll probably start a new one in Florida. I can't believe I finally filled a journal up—I never thought I'd see the day!

And I still can't believe Sam and I had sex. Even though it was the longest, weirdest day, the memory still feels like this little shining bubble of joy inside me, making me happy wherever I go.

I lost my virginity. And I feel fine. Not scared, or dirty, or broken, or tainted or like I "regret this notch on my bedpost."

Author's Note

Phoebe's Diary is a fictionalized adaptation of my real-life high school diaries, from 2006 to 2007. If you are wondering how much of the book is "real," the answer is nebulous. While I drew from my own diaries, there is no passage or character left unchanged in some way. However, all the *feelings* in this book are very real.

When I was a teenager, I thought there was something wrong with me for being curious about sex and having a body larger than the ones I saw reflected in the media. It's taken me many years to realize that the problem is not with *me*, but with society's fatphobia and sex negativity, and the constant, unrelenting ways it teaches us to be ashamed of our bodies and what we want to do with them. I sometimes wish I could go back and protect my younger self from the negative ways I was taught to think. And at first, I felt the inclination to protect my readers from them too.

But I wanted to be honest about my emotional experiences, which meant including the painful parts, the cringey bits, the internalized self-doubt, and other truths that were a part of my life. I think there is a lot of power in being open about these stigmas. They fuel judgment and warp our relationships with ourselves and others. And while it is difficult, it *is* possible to learn to reject the lies we are told—and to trust instead that all bodies deserve justice, love, and respect, including yours.

Acknowledgments

There are so many people who helped me make this book. Foremost, my fifteen-year-old self, whose mortifyingly honest, unparalleled romanticism and angst made this book what it is—you can blame her for all the raunchiest, cringiest parts. My adult self couldn't have made them up even if I tried.

Thank you to Jennifer Laughran for welcoming this manuscript so wholeheartedly, when I felt so vulnerable and embarrassed to be showing it to anyone. Thank you to my visionary editor, Susan Rich, for holding this project and encouraging it to grow with so much love and trust and tenderness. Thank you to all the hero designers who had to wade through and make sense of my hundreds of doodles of corn dogs and bras and flip phones—Sasha Illingworth, Patrick Hulse, and Neil Swaab. And everyone else behind the scenes at Little, Brown, thank you for helping bring this book to life.

Thank you to DH, for workshopping outside on cold pandemic nights, I'm so grateful to have you as a memory keeper and friend. Thank you, B, for your openness and trust, and to all the real-life friends, teachers, loved ones, and strangers who inspired bits of the fictional characters in this book. Thank you to my sister for being my fierce protector, even when it was imperfect. You are and always will be my top influencer, confidant, and best friend. I love you, but I still don't regret all the notches on my bedpost, bitch! Thank you to Emmy for being my cottonwood tree. Thank you to Rob, the owner of Trek Video (RIP) for sending me reference photos so I could get it just right for the few who will care. Thank you, Bow, for being my top Bellingham and Myspace history consultant. Thank you to the real-life Olivia Wormwood—I'm eternally grateful that you showed me an example of fat style and joy when I needed it most.

Thank you to my childcare team, Mom, Ingrid, and Wendy, for taking care of Hazel while I worked. Especially Mom, for being my biggest cheerleader even when I'm making something that probably makes her want to run away and hide in a cave. Thank you to my therapist, and thank you to Maddie, Stephanie, Mal, and Han for kicking ass always but especially during this wild time. And last but not least, thank you to my husband, Peter, for waiting so patiently on the other side of the creative void while I disappeared for days on end, for making sure I was eating and drinking and getting sleep, for showing me how to draw drum sets and bongs, for holding me and being patient with me through the ups and downs of making this book during a pandemic, a pregnancy, and new parenthood. You have been an exemplary co-parent and partner through this process. I love you so much.

MORE YA NOVELS FROM
SHADOW MOUNTAIN

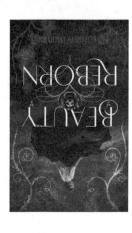

"An intriguing, well-crafted original..."
—*Kirkus Reviews*

"A sensitive and slow-burning retelling."
—*Publishers Weekly*

"Undeniable chemistry propels this amorous tale to a satisfyingly romantic resolution."
—*Publishers Weekly*

Cursed by magic, bound by mistakes, Princess Aria finds her destiny hinges on the mysterious Baron Reeves. Will love be enough to break the curse, or will war bring her kingdom to ruin?

SHADOW
MOUNTAIN